Got Love If You Want It
(17 May 1964)

Christopher Thomason

HAWKWOOD & LANE

Got Love If You Want It
(17 May 1964)

Second Edition, 2015

Published Worldwide by Hawkwood & Lane,
Chislehurst, England

Copyright © Christopher Thomason, 2014

By Christopher Thomason:

Got Love If You Want It (17 May 1964)

For The Want Of Beauty

Contents:

Got Love If You Want It
(17 May 1964)

People try to put us down
Just because we get around
Things they do look awful cold
I hope I die before I get old

My Generation
The Who

Chapter 1

Jimmy gave the machine a loving pat, wiping the early morning dew from the seat and handle grips before stepping on. It was 4am. Usually he'd stay another half hour or so. Sally's old man was never home before five. But he wanted to get a few hours sleep before they all met up and headed south.

He was excited, of course he was. Yeah, and also a bit apprehensive. Mikey had been very straight - and tense - the other night. We're going down because that's the right thing for us to do, he said. Meaning he was sick of having to listen to those East Ham and Barking boys praising themselves up for kicking a few old greasers out at Clacton.

Mind you, Mikey had tried to insist, we're not going to do anything stupid. If all that turns up with us are posh wasters from places like Wimbledon and Chislehurst then we turn around and get back. No silly heroics. Our time will come.

Well, that was the talk but it was tosh. Mikey was as keen to be a part of heroics and glory as the rest of them. Keen for a bit of fame. A reputation. A legend of their own that would make heads turn and voices lower next time they walked in The Roaring Twenties.

Sally was standing by the door still, wearing nothing but some old shirt. Well, her neighbours were her concern, he couldn't be worrying for her if she wasn't worried for herself. He waved, blew her a kiss, kicked the thing into buzzing life and eased away down towards the Rye, passing his old primary school with its new playground.

As he swung round behind the station he noticed a light on in Bowles' garage, which seemed odd but not odd enough for him to stop and check. The place was like a fortress so there was no chance anyone had got in. Maybe Keith was polishing up his TV. It was already the number 1 machine in south London. Totally perfect in cream and dark green, with gleaming chrome running boards, wings and back rest, plus four mirrors on these fabulously curved stalks. Or maybe he'd scored with that cute redhead he'd been fussing around up at The Scene.

Jimmy slipped quietly into his house, took the stairs as silently as he could and closed the door to his room like it was made of glass. The arguments with his parents had pretty much burned themselves out now. They were far more worried about his sister, fifteen, pretty and just starting to get a little wild. She was clever and all that, but too trusting. Some of those girls she hung with were going to be tarts because that's how their mothers had been. One still was according to Pete.

He had talked to her. They got on OK. Better than most he reckoned. She was adamant she wasn't going that way and he believed her. But the point was, he'd tried to make her see, it didn't matter what she did. It was what people thought she did that counted. Having a slag's reputation was like getting dog shit stuck in the soles of your shoes. You didn't meant to tread in it, but you stink all the same.

He hung up his latest suit with care - a simple dark blue three-button, with a shawl collar and chequered lining old Bilgorri in Bishopsgate had made him, copying the latest Brioni from a magazine. He'd been thinking of wearing it later, but that would be dumb really. There was going to be action, he was sure of that. No sense getting his best gear ripped. So, he pulled out the dark grey mohair he'd got off-the-peg from Take Six in February, together with a pale blue Brooks Brothers shirt he couldn't leave off a couple of months ago, but which he'd lately been thinking of relegating to work-wear.

Then the uppers wore off and tiredness hit. He lay back on his bed and, with the taste of Sally still on his tongue, fell asleep.

It was 9am when he woke. Or rather, was woken. The tone of his mother's voice suggested it was only her third call. It was loud, but sent up from the bottom of the stairs with no curses. Worse, much worse would follow if he didn't get moving. Then again, the smell of eggs and bacon was enough to get him up.

He wished he hadn't fallen asleep in his best shirt though. Two guineas from Austin's in Shaftesbury Avenue. The thing was crumpled up like an old dishcloth now. He took it off and hung it up with apologetic respect, slipping himself into the hideous tartan dressing gown his aunt Florrie had bought last Christmas. Well, no-one was going to see him.

"Bit late last night weren't we?" his mother asked over her shoulder from the cooker, her lips pursed with fake anger.

"Were you?" Jimmy replied with a smile, his head leaning to one side to feign both interest and surprise. "Well don't worry, you didn't wake me. They wake you Janey?"

"Never heard them," his sister replied deadpan without looking up from her allotted task of buttering the bread.

"I meant you, wise-arse."

"Me?" he asked with wide-eyed shock. "No way, in well early ..." he insisted, standing by the sink, filling a glass with water.

"So what did I hear getting on for five?"

"How do I know?" he shrugged, gulping the water as he headed over to join his sister and father at the table. "Perhaps next door's cat?"

"Yeah, yeah," his mum smiled, dishing up the first two plates - one egg, two rashers, one sausage, a few fried up old potatoes. "You want beans Billy?"

"Now steady dad, you know your trouble ..." Jimmy teased, leaning back quickly to avoid getting the Sunday Mirror slapping against his ears.

"So, when we going to get to meet this girl of yours?" his father asked while answering his wife with a simple thumbs up.

"Well dad, you see, the thing is, it's complicated. She's like this Doctor guy. You know, a Time Traveller. So ..."

"Thought of buying her a watch?" Billy suggested laconically while shaking the bottle of HP. "Kitty," he beamed, looking up at his wife as the plates got laid down, "that looks perfect as always," he determined, patting the woman playfully on her bottom.

"Didn't think much of yesterday's," Jane put in randomly while getting up to fetch the tea - her second job.

"Sorry?" he asked of his daughter, handing the HP bottle over to his son, a large dollop of the stuff now resting in the crater of one rasher of well-done bacon.

"Doctor Who. It was silly."

"I thought it was quite good," her mother replied, a slight look of hurt on her face.

"Yeah, well," the girl giggled, getting the milk from the larder.

"Now what's that supposed to mean?"

"Mum, it's like that copper you like. Dixon. You know he's going to get whoever did it so what's the point?"

"So what do you think the point is then?" Billy asked, his mouth half full.

"I just think it's time people made stuff for the telly that looks more real."

"Yeah, well, if you ask me, some of those plays they puts on now are too real," Kitty sighed, dishing up her and Jane's plates.

"So what you reading at school right now then?" Jimmy asked.

"Pinter. Just done the Birthday Party. Doing the Caretaker next."

"Hmm," Jimmy nodded, impressed. "Serious stuff. You like all that?"

"Yeah, I do. I'd like to write, I think. That would be good, don't you think?"

"Actually, I do. You keep at it," her brother nodded, his mind already predicting the problems - of expectation as well as confidence - she would run into if she was serious: Peckham girls don't write books.

"I saw that Penny Carr," Kitty put in, the value of realistic drama lost on her.

"Really, where?" Jimmy asked, wiping his plate clean with a slice of bread.

"In Jones and Higgins. Lovely girl, really lovely girl."

"Yeah, well I agree with you there mum."

"There you go then," Kitty nodded conspiratorially.

"There I go where?" Jimmy laughed, pouring out the teas.

"Maybe, you know, a girl like Penny … she likes you, I could tell that easy."

"Yeah, she also likes Mikey, who happens to be my best mate!" Jimmy replied, laughing with exasperation now.

"She's too good for him."

"Mum, I know you're not keen on him."

"He always was a terror, at school and since … course, his father was no good."

"True," Billy nodded over his blue and white striped mug.

"So you've told me."

"Well, no point denying it," Kitty insisted.

"Actually, he doesn't. Mikey can't stand his dad."

"Is that right? I didn't realise," Billy put in thoughtfully, his eyes holding his son's.

"Well, I don't think he has much to do with him now. But all this stuff you've said before about Paddy O'Dea. You know, ducked out of the war. Made lots of money as a spiv … Mikey knows all that. He ain't proud of it."

"No, well …" Billy nodded, "guess I'd not thought about that before. Can't have been easy for the boy. You know, sins of the father."

"You sticking up for him now Billy Carlton?"

"No, not as such. But maybe you are a bit hard on the boy Kitty. I mean, it's not his fault his dad's no good. And he does work himself, don't he?"

"GPO. Earns good money," Jimmy nodded.

"Yeah, well … say one thing for Paddy O'Dea. Got me a ticket for the '45 Cup Final."

"So he should have," Kitty put in sharply. "You'd only just come out of hospital, couldn't walk properly. Least the little shit could have done."

"Mum," Jimmy laughed. "Is it me, or don't you like him?"

"Don't get smart with me. I ain't going with your father on this. Paddy O'Dea was no good."

"What you talking about?" Billy asked with a little exasperation. "I agree with you! Don't mean I wasn't happy to take that ticket though. Last time Millwall got close to winning anything."

"You want my bet?" Jimmy said. "They'll get promoted next season, bounce straight back."

"You reckon?"

"Yeah, definite. And I'll try and get to some more games with you, promise," he smiled, enjoying the easy way his father's optimism rose, even if all the evidence suggested their team was one of life's lost causes. Then again, that was the thing about football. It wasn't the disappointment that killed you, it was the hope.

"Says she works with this girl," Kitty said.

"Sorry, who does?" Jane asked.

"Penny. Works with this time travelling girl."

"My, didn't you two talk," Jimmy smiled ruefully.

"Like I said, she's nice. Says you's all off to Brighton today, that right?"

"Er, yeah," he replied, not wanting this conversation.

"Yeah, well that's my point. You stay out of trouble, you hear."

"Too right," Billy echoed. "No way is that Michael O'Dea going to be any help."

"Hold on, just a minute ago you were alright about him," Jimmy snapped.

"I said it's not his fault his father was a spiv," Billy nodded philosophically. "But bravery and looking out for others, that's another matter. That's hereditary. You'll find all that in those Greek books you used to like reading."

"So how d'you know about that stuff?"

"I went to school too you know," Billy smiled. "Now come on, we've got washing up to do."

Jimmy watched his father carefully from the corner of his eye. This had been their Sunday morning ritual since he was about ten. A lesson in the ways of family harmony and respect: his father washed, he dried and put away, while his mother got to sit down and listen to the radio.

There had been times when he had truly believed he hated Billy Carlton, for not being able to get this or for making him do something he didn't want. But the bottom line was, deep down he'd always known he was a decent man. A good man. A quiet man, yes - except for the two or three times a year he downed too many black and tans. And, at times, a stubborn and humourless man. But mostly, he was cheerful and contented. Happy in his work and proud of his little family.

All of which also meant there was a certain mystery about him. Jimmy knew little about his father's childhood. Partly because his grandfather - the usual source of embarrassing stories - died when he was eight. But mostly, he had worked out - as the years rolled on and he became more attuned to the subtleties in his father's character - the mystery lay in the one subject he simply did not talk about: his war.

And, no matter others might not get the logic, Jimmy felt he understood that meant not talking about the time before the war either. Why? Maybe because that would mean talking about people who didn't survive. Or maybe, because talking about moments of lightness and happiness before 1939 would make it harder to keep the memories of the six years that followed shuffled away in some dark cupboard in his mind. So today's few comments about Paddy O'Dea represented as much as his father had said on those war years in a long time.

His mother had always been different on the subject. But then again, that wasn't so hard to understand. She'd been left behind. Married one week, abandoned the next by a man she would only then see for a few odd weeks in the best part of five years before he came home half-dead and half-crippled.

The spirit amongst those that stayed was, when all was said and done, uplifting. Worth sharing - even if his mother and her sisters tended to over-share! By contrast, the experiences of those that went away were too depressing to bear retelling.

But then, what had he meant by that reference to ancient Greek literature? Fair enough, Jimmy remembered his dad buying him a new pair of football boots to prove how proud he was of his son getting in a school adaptation of the Odyssey, even though all he had was a bit-part in the Phaeacian Games. But beyond that he couldn't recall any other moment of interest.

The man was a furniture maker, the son of one, brother of another! What did he know of Homer?

Yet he wasn't wrong. Be better than your father - be faster, stronger, braver, smarter - that was what the gods demanded of their heroes. Poor old Diomedes - who had been Jimmy's hero for a while - had battled away against Trojans all day. He sat down for a moment, wounded and knackered and instantly had Athene on his case telling him he was a coward who didn't deserve to be Tydeus' son, Oeneus' grandson. Still, that worked. He was up again in no time, taking husbands from their wives, fathers from their children, splitting bodies from their souls.

For those guys there was only one thing worse than a useless, profitless life and that was an inglorious death.

Perhaps his dad had read Homer or Herodotus or Thucydides during all the sitting around waiting? Borrowed the books from an officer or something. Maybe a little of it had hit home. Maybe that was what gave Billy Carlton that sense of presence no-one could deny he had.

He wasn't a tall guy. Maybe a little above average but seeing as he walked with a pronounced limp you wouldn't see it. But he was solid and when he stared hard people gave way. Why? Maybe because they saw behind those eyes a man content with the knowledge he did his bit. He gave of his best. He wasn't found wanting.

Sure, soon enough he would start to get properly old. Start to stoop. Start to stutter, lose his hair, think three times before telling some young turk to shut the fuck up. But that self-regard would be there till the day he died.

Yeah. And now, at last, Jimmy understood his own birth. He'd been told about the 1945 Cup Final before. Of course he had. But as always, Millwall lost. But maybe that didn't matter. All that mattered was Billy'd had a great day out; followed by a good night in.

Yep, it certainly fitted together. That game was 7 April 1945. He'd been born January 5th, 1946. Come on you Lions!

"You know dad, Jane, she's alright …"

"Course she is son …"

"No, I'm being serious, she's … well, she's smart."

"I know. Your mother … well, she worries about some of these other girls. Them Freeman sisters especially."

"They say their mother was a right slag."

"Yeah, well, they don't say wrong. Maddy Terry, that was her name then. Maddy Terry Always Ready, that's what they said."

"I also heard her husband left her."

"After he found her shagging his best mate? Yep. So I make you right boy about this Penny Carr. And I don't know, maybe the Freeman girls are OK. I mean, like you were saying about your friend, people change. Families change … happened with them old Greeks, didn't it?"

"Hmm," Jimmy pondered. "Not so sure really. Orestes, he did manage to lift the family curse …"

"Oh yeah?"

"Killed his mother 'cos she'd killed his father, then went mad."

"Happy folk then!" Billy laughed.

"Exactly! I don't know them dad, the Freeman twins. So like you say, maybe they are OK. But their mother's still no good I hear. Pete reckons his dad goes round."

"Wouldn't surprise me. He was never a picky man that Alfie Bowles."

"No, but anyway," Jimmy continued seriously. "About Jane. I did talk to her. She understands. No way is she going to be like that anyway and I think she understands how much it matters what people think. You know, that she can't let herself get the same reputation as them."

"You said all that?" Billy asked, impressed and proud.

"Yeah, why not? She's my sister," Jimmy insisted, misunderstanding his father's tone.

"I wasn't saying you shouldn't have son. I was saying thanks."

"Oh right, yeah, well, like I said …"

"She's your sister," Billy nodded, smiling.

"That's right. So the thing I really wanted to say was, I think she might want to stay on at school. You know, do A-levels, maybe …"

"Why didn't you?"

"Me?"

"Yeah, why didn't you? You were clever, got into grammar school like her."

"Well, truth is dad, I'm not sure I have a great answer on that. I don't regret it as such. I like the bank. It's good money. They like me. I could do OK. But sometimes I do wonder … guess the truth is I kind of talked myself out of it."

"Sorry son, not working for me. This more greek?"

"I guess I just thought kids like me, from round here I mean, we get out to work. I was already thinking I was taking the piss staying on till I was sixteen …"

"But I never said a word," Billy interrupted, a little put out.

"No, you didn't. You never did. So no way am I blaming you or mum. I stopped myself. That's my point, I stopped myself … but maybe …"

"Maybe what?" Billy asked quietly.

"Maybe, if you'd said something like 'you know what son, pointless you getting to this school and not making the most of it …' something like that, well then maybe I …"

"So you're saying I should say something like that to Jane."

"Yes dad. Yes I am. I think it could make the difference. Make all the difference. You don't have to say you want her to be a writer or any of that. That might just be a thing with her at the moment. But she's worth something better than hairdressing or shop work, don't you think?"

"Well, as it happens, I do," Billy smiled, putting his arm around his son's shoulder, hugging him close. "Not sure your mother does mind. Think she'd rather like a discount in Jones and Higgins!"

Chapter 2

I'm going down the road
Stop at Fannie Mae's
Gonna tell Fannie
What I've heard her boyfriend say
Don't start me that talking
I'll tell everything I know
Gonna break up this signifying
Everybody's got to go.

Don't Start Me Talking
Sonny Boy Williams

They met up out front of The Dog in Dulwich Village.

Michael and Penny were already there, standing next to his nearly-new Li 150 Special, bought off a rich cat from Denmark Hill who'd barely done 200 miles in six months. White with red side panels and wheels, a red and white double seat and this gorgeous chrome back rest with a blue / white / red target cushion.

Mikey wore a nice enough blue suit. Well, maybe a bit Lord John in truth and a shade or two too bright, but it looked OK with a white shirt, black tie and oxblood loafers. Penny though just looked so great in a pair of Prince of Wales check slacks, white socks and black flats, with a black cardigan over a round-collar white blouse. More than that, the way she now wore her dark hair - short and tufty just like Jean Seberg - suited her so well.

Next to them were Manny Weinstein and Dawn Pearson. He was a big guy, six foot and broad with it. He had good taste and sold decent enough stuff off his stall down East Lane. Yet at the same time he always looked like a donkey in a tuxedo. It wasn't that he didn't get stuff to fit. It was just that he never looked quite right in it. Still,

Jimmy was envious of his red Harrington. Had that on his list for next time he had some cash to spare.

Dawn, bless her, tried. But next to Penny she looked too dumpy and just a little cheap. Her white slacks were far too tight on the hips, her jumper too tight for her over-large breasts, while her patent-leather shoes were just too 1962. She knew it though, deep down, you could tell. Well, she'd been at school with Penny so'd had plenty of time to get used to it. And Manny's gold and silver Vespa did look good, even if it was a mystery to Jimmy why anyone would want anything but a Lambretta.

As he parked up he saw a little convoy coming down the hill. Up front was Pete Bowles on his LD150. Colour apart it was identical to Jimmy's own. Pete's dad had picked up the pair - one a '58 the other a '59 - cheap but pretty much wrecked. Jimmy had no idea how many hours of work went into the two scooters, but it must have been over the hundred. The result was two better then new machines.

Jimmy had picked the older thinking that might cost a little less, but seeing as Alfie wouldn't take a penny off him he might as well have gone for the '59. He was glad he didn't though. Having been uncertain to start with, he now thought the cream and blue a much better look than Pete's cream and maroon.

Behind Pete was Stevie Dolan, one of Mikey's mates from work, with Penny's sixteen year old brother Toby on the back. Stevie was a decent fella but he was no face. Just didn't really have the feel for it. Never quite had the right clothes, couldn't dance and wasn't much use in a fight. All of which was probably why Penny had decided he'd be perfect to carry Toby. The way he drove his LD125 - basically like a vicar - there was no way the two of them would get down before it was all over.

Shotgun was Keith Thomas, the main mechanic at Bowles' garage and a well cool dude with it. His TV had the lot: 175cc; four gears; ten inch wheels; fabulously curved side panels with chrome lined air vents; running boards all the way down; a fancy red and orange brake light; four mirrors, two spots and an Innocenti crested badge. Plus, the speedo went up to 100mph, even if the machine itself didn't!

The nine of them stood around chatting for a while. Joshing about this, ribbing each other for that and generally avoiding the leaving. Mikey was sure they'd meet up with some decent guys from Forest Hill on the way down. Jimmy said he knew some Clapham faces were going. Keith said his cousin from Hammersmith had telephoned first thing to say there were half a dozen of them. Pete said it didn't matter, no-one was gonna mess with Big Manny, who pulled some macho wrestler pose to prove the point.

Dawn was OK about it all, not silly keen but accepting that they had to do what they had to do. But Penny said very little. She looked a little tense really, probably because she was looking out for her kid brother, Jimmy thought.

Then, as they were all walking to the scooters she hung back off Mikey a moment till the two of them were as good as alone. She gazed at him hard with her hazel eyes, the golden halo around her black pupils shining like the sun during an eclipse. "Listen," she whispered while holding his arm, "don't you dare get hurt Jimmy Carlton, you hear."

Jimmy had paused a moment, staring back, trying to work out why she seemed so worried. He couldn't. So he just smiled back as reassuringly as he could and said: "Course, you don't have to fret about me."

And that was it. Coats and hats on - save for Stevie who wore a helmet; fair enough, it was a Guzzi, but he still looked a complete haddock - and they were off.

The crash was just the stupidest, stupidest thing. He really wasn't being that lairy or anything like it. Sure, it had all got a bit boring. They'd been on the road, stopping and starting, for hours. It was all going to be over by the time they got there. But by then they'd met up with plenty of cool people and the weather had perked up. It was looking like it'd be a good afternoon.

He and Pete had actually dropped away from Mikey and the rest to ride with a couple of faces they'd got to know lately at the Crawdaddy out in Richmond: Charlie and Jon, Clapham boys. They both had quite average scooters, but great taste.

Jon especially. He had this mop of unruly black hair flowing from beneath his pork pie hat, a double-breasted jacket, kind of military looking, houndstooth check strides and a pair of suede loafers from Pinnays. Cost seven guineas. Totally cool.

Charlie was less original: dark suit, black Chelsea boots and a fishtail parka. But his shirt was really special: a deep-red button-down with a faint blue check. Got it from Courtney Reeds.

A couple of months back the four of them had met up Sunday afternoon and gone down to the club expecting to see the Stones again, only to find they were off for the week. Instead this band called The Kinks were on. Nowhere near as good, save for one song: Got Love If You Want It. They really did this great. So great in fact they did it three times as Charlie remembered it.

Anyway, so the four of them had sung that while riding along. Then belted out a few other R&B favourites while admiring the countryside. So green. So empty save for some sheep one side of the road, a few wild horses running free in a field to their left. So unlike London.

Then, at last, they saw the crest of the South Downs. Soon be there, world look out. Cue for a reprise of Got Love with Jimmy on mimed harmonica - which is probably why he fell off. Not that he was going to admit that to anyone, no way - too fucking embarrassing.

When he came to he had that many people leaning over he thought it must be night, they were totally blocking the light. His head hurt like crazy and he couldn't move his left leg or left arm. Well, actually he couldn't move his right side much either but it felt as though that would be alright in a moment, as soon as he got his mind together. But the left side was completely numb.

He tried to lift his head to look back, to see how far it had been. He couldn't, but at least it was all coming back now. Stupid not to have kept both hands on the handlebars, totally stupid. He wouldn't do that again. Just hadn't realised how quickly things can go wrong.

One second he's Ray Davies giving it huge on the pretend mouth organ. The next the front tyre hits a crack in the road, slips a little to the left making the rear spin out the other way and before he's got control he's going sideways. Halfway toppled. The tarmac ripping through the dark grey mohair before doing the same to the skin around his left knee.

He must have passed out as he slid along. Just as well he hadn't worn the blue faux-Brioni. He would have been seriously pissed off if he'd shredded that.

And his scooter. The noise had been horrible. Smashing his mirrors and scrapping off the paint with a shrill screech, like the sound of dirty chalk on a blackboard.

He remembered him and that Davie what's-his-name at school deliberately dirtying the chalks of the RE teacher, what was his name … Father Peters, that was him. Couldn't write up a thing with them! Oh yeah, and there was that time they'd all been giving him a hard time, messing around, answering back and the silly old git had said: every time I open my mouth a fool speaks. Too true, make you right there Sir!

"I told you. I fucking told you," he heard Penny saying. Her voice seemed weak and upset, but she was busying herself with a wet handkerchief around his bleeding knee.

"You alright kiddo?" Mikey asked.

"Yeah, he's coming round now," Manny reckoned.

"Thank fuck," Jimmy heard Charlie say, although he couldn't actually see him, the sound seemed to come from behind his head and he was still finding the job of moving anything a major trial.

"Anyone got any water or anything?" Mikey asked, looking around randomly.

Toby had this cycling bottle. They wet his lips from that. Poured a little in his mouth, made him choke a bit but that wasn't a bad thing, all part of bringing him round.

Toby was a decent kid, fancied himself a smart number in his white cycling shirt, pale-blue v-neck and black Sta-Prest. He looked a lot like his sister. Same eyes, similar features, same dark hair which she'd cut for him so it was like he had proper long sideburns, with an over-the-collar length at the back but just as short as hers on top. It was well neat. That said, he seemed a bit fucked-up, a bit queasy or something. Maybe that Stevie Dolan's riding was racier than Jimmy had imagined? Nah, more likely the kid was just embarrassed at having to sit on an LD125.

"Come on man," Jon seemed to be saying. Jimmy couldn't hear him as such because of the banging in his head, just caught the sense from the way his lips moved. His dark eyes were staring really, really hard through that thick fringe of his. Didn't have his hat on now. No-one but no-one had hair like Jon. Well, maybe that guitarist in The Birds but he was too fucking ugly to be taken seriously.

Jon was a good looking guy, no denying that. He could handle himself too. Jimmy had seen him. Some arse had been giving him a load of verbal, calling him a poof because of his tight strides and baggy shirt. Two punches: one to line him up, the second to knock him spark-o. The guy must have been six inches taller than Jon easy, yet he didn't have a chance.

That was it, though. That was what they were all wanting to be. Jimmy didn't think he was too shabby either. Didn't bother him how big they were. Hit anyone hard enough on the chin and they're over, simple. But you had to have the look too. You had to have attitude. Dress good, dance great and fight hard.

Where was Jon's jacket? He had on the identical shirt to Jimmy's latest Austin's - slim fit, small rounded collar, mother of pearl buttons - but in black. So cool. Jimmy had seen that when he bought his. Thought long about it, but in the end went easy and took the white. That was the thing about Jon, he didn't just take the easy. Dead opposite actually. He wanted to be the first to try this, wear that. Then move on again before anyone caught up. But where was his jacket? Jimmy wondered before realising that it was laying across his chest, like a blanket or something.

Fucking hell, he thought, I'm getting treated like a girl here. He tried to push the jacket off, feeling himself weighed down like Odysseus after he'd been tossed from his boat, dragged deep by crashing waves and twisting currents.

He choked again as Mikey poured more water into his mouth, spitting some over Jon's coat as he tried for some air.

"OK, OK," he gasped.

Once he'd got to his feet, staggered around a bit apologising to one and all, he took a look at his scooter. He didn't really need Keith and Pete to tell him it was unrideable. It wasn't just the scarring all down the nearside, nor the smashed-up mirrors. Nor the burst front tyre - he had a spare after all. It was obvious even to him that something was well wrong with the front end.

Keith explained that the forks were bent, they'd have to be rebuilt. New rods and dampers - whatever they were - also. Pete promised the two of them would come down with his dad's truck, take it back and put it all right for him. Might take a month or so but they'd do it.

Definitely, Keith nodded, no question, it can be made good again, for sure.

In truth, Jimmy wasn't so very disappointed. He really didn't feel he would have been up to riding anyway. His left arm still felt totally numb. All he could really do was hold it across his chest, his wrist resting on a fastened button to his jacket, his hand inside. Like Napoleon.

At least he could move his fingers a little now, and the pain from where the skin had been torn off around his knee at least said he was on the mend! His right side was sort of OK now. The bits of gravel buried in his right palm hurt. He'd maybe get to wash those out in the sea, though, he thought. No point worrying about his trousers any more so he might as well wade in and wash his cuts in the salty water, that should sort things out.

Keith's scooter did feel powerful. Whereas his own always wheezed going up hill - like an asthmatic in a pea souper - the TV just seemed to glide along as though it had power to spare. Well, as far as he understood it, the thing did. Had a decent engine plus that extra gear makes a big difference, evidently. So he leaned back against the tall and rather comfortable rear cushion and watched the world speed by.

As they went over the top of the South Downs he saw the sea shimmering in the far distance. The sun was high and a little off centre now, which seemed to add magic to the sparkle dancing across the water, making the foam topping each wave shine with tiny points of light, like the Christmas tree the Norwegians always put up in Trafalgar Square.

They were starting to leave the countryside behind. Starting to meet small collections of nice-looking houses, all with big gardens and a decent car in the driveway. One day Jimmy Carlton, he told himself.

Yeah, one day. One day when he'd maybe lived a little more. Done a few more things. Got respect as a top face. Put himself in good with the top men at the bank.

Yeah, he needed to do both those things, do them together. Gaining more and more respect was how you built more and more self-confidence. Offer yourself to the world confident and content and you get taken seriously, moved up, made manager and all that useful shit.

Making your own luck, that was what it was all about. Making your own luck, not taking it for granted. It's no good feeling super high when everything's going your way and then lower than a sausage dog's belly when you hit a bad spot.

Yeah, that was it, who was that guy … Boethius, yeah, him. Fortune is fickle, that's just how she is. The thing is not to take it personally. Not to think she's picked you out as a favourite when the dice fall your way or decided you're a bozo when the tables turn. It's what you do that counts. What you do and who sees you do it. Yeah, and that was the other thing: you never really knew yourself till you'd had Fortune turn against you.

Jimmy was tempted for a moment to think that was what had happened to him. That while he'd been busy taking a chance with all that singing and miming he'd forgotten to check how full his jar of luck was. Forgotten to watch out for what Lady Fortune was up to.

Then he realised the Lady hadn't turned against him at all. Sure, he wished he hadn't fallen off. Wished he hadn't trashed his scooter. Wished he hadn't ripped his suit. Wished his head would stop pounding.

But all of those things were just details. Irritants yes, but it could have been worse. His life was still ahead of him. Opportunity was still ahead of him.

That was the thing, wasn't it. Always look forward, not back. Always expectant, never regretful. You can't change the past so forget it.

That was where Odysseus got it all wrong when he thought Poseidon was about to drag him under. Sure, dying alone at sea wouldn't have been an especially glorious way to go. But to think everything would have been better if he'd just died on the battlefield with his comrades, well that was missing the point.

It's not the drama or setting of the dying that counts, it's the quality of the life. Nations remember their dead for what they did, not how they fell.

But maybe Odysseus was speaking to a different feeling, the guilt carried by those that survive? Quite rightly, people remember those who died doing their bit. But they give honours to the still living. Of course they do. It makes them feel proud and safe knowing there are heroes walking amongst them.

But how do those newly announced heroes really feel inside? How did Billy Carlton feel? Was he troubled at times by the thought he could have done more? That those he left behind are the true heroes because they gave the lot?

Leave it all on the pitch, that's what Turner used to drum into them at school. The worse feeling in the world is to walk off beaten knowing you had more to give.

Great game, rugby. Jimmy hadn't expected to like it. Not at all. Almost gave up the chance to go to St Olave's because of it. Thought maybe the new comprehensive where Pete was going, where Mikey and Manny were already might be better: new buildings, big fields and they played football.

He was glad he hadn't. Glad for lots of reasons and one of them was the rugby - war without weapons. Leave it all on the pitch Carlton!

His dad didn't need to feel guilty. He nearly did leave it all out there in the desert. That he came home more dead than alive said he hadn't been looking out for himself. No, he'd given the lot and been smart enough not to let his jar of luck run empty.

Great image that old Boethius had: we all start out with a jar of good luck and a jar of bad. Fortune has a lot to say about how those jars get emptied, so you got to show her respect. But don't leave it at that. Don't let her have it all her own way. Look after those jars. Look after them well and sometimes it will feel like you're making a little of your own good luck.

So, for all that he'd just fucked some of that up, Jimmy felt the Lady was still with him. She'd taught him a lesson. Too right she had. But now he'd thought about it, learned from it, it was time to move on. Move on and become the kind of guy he wanted to be. Wanted to be remembered for being. The kind that does the right thing for the right reason.

And as soon as his head stopped pounding that was exactly what he was going to do. He was going to have a good life, he felt sure of it. He was going to make it happen. But right now the pounding in his head was starting to make him dizzy and nauseous.

Then again, at least he felt he could move his left hand a little, move it enough. He reached into the inside pocket of his jacket. Fished a heart-shaped pill out of the small envelope there. Popping it into his mouth, he crunched it up and swallowed the bits with saliva. Not exactly a glamorous way to score but even so, the hit soon worked through. Worked through, pushing the throbbing out of his mind and the aching out of his limbs, replacing hurt with a warm, bright, comforting lightness.

Chapter 3

I don't like you, but I love you
Seems that I'm always thinking of you
Oh, oh-o-o, you treat me badly
I love you madly
You've really got a hold on me.

You Really Got A Hold On Me
Smokey Robinson

By the time they reached Brighton Pavilion the whole area was full of Mods from different parts of London and the South. Many, especially those from the counties, had their little town in letters on their scooters and parkas.

Others were distinguishable just from the clothes they wore. The Crawley and Guildford guys were mainly Levi Mods, comfortable in jeans, roll-necks and desert boots. The east London and Medway boys tended to favour tonic, braces and Fred Perry. The south and west London faces were mostly in top quality jackets or suits, shirts and shoes.

Leaders of the different groups met beneath the portico in front of the main onion dome. The rest hung around in different clusters, some talking and laughing with people they'd met at clubs, gigs or just out and about. Others sticking together moodily.

Still feeling below par, Jimmy sat down on the grass and gazed back at the strangely beautiful, if now more than a little neglected and derelict, old palace. He was no great student of architecture, but then again you didn't have to be to marvel at the imagination that could come up with something like this.

They must have had some seriously good hash, he chuckled to himself, his eyes flowing along the roof line: around one onion dome, up and down a minaret, up and over some conical clown's hat type thing, then more domes, more minarets, then another clown's hat and a dome to match the first. It was classical decorated with a weird confection of twists and turns, spires and arches, mosaics and carvings.

"You are one lucky so-and-so," Penny smiled, sitting down next to him.

"I guess," Jimmy nodded. "If you call a throbbing head, ripped suit and trashed scooter lucky …"

"Yes, I do," she insisted. "What were you doing?"

"Nothing, not really. I guess the truth is, I just wasn't taking enough care. Sorry," he shrugged in rueful apology.

"Yeah, well," she accepted, looking up at the gathering by the Pavilion. "All a lot of Boy's Own crap this, though, isn't it?"

"Don't let Mikey hear you talk like that," he suggested.

"Oh, he knows what I think!"

"Yeah, I bet he does," Jimmy nodded with admiring respect, a wry grin on his face. "So why'd you come Penny?"

"Keep an eye on the lot of you," she smiled. "Besides, it'll just be a bit of yah-booing then we can all go dancing or something."

"Oh yeah. Whatever happens, we'll go dancing," he agreed, his headache starting to clear.

"Girl at our place, lives out near Barking, or somewhere like that. She says this big thing at Clacton that soppy-arse …"

"Soppy-arse?"

"Yeah, Mr O … what was it you used to call him?"

"Odysseus."

"Yeah. Why? He was some kind of hero wasn't he?"

"Some say. Others wonder about a dude whose men either got turned into pigs, eaten by monsters or lost at sea!"

"Oh, right!" Penny chuckled. "Well, do yourself a favour Jimmy, don't go trusting Mikey to lead you."

"You kidding me?" Jimmy laughed. "He's my mate and all that, but you wouldn't want to get in a fight and find he's all you've got on your side!"

"So why do you all go letting him think he's like Top Cat?"

"Does no harm. Makes him feel good. Doesn't take anything away from the rest of us. What's the worry?"

"My, I do believe that bump on the head has done you some good Jimmy Carlton."

"Why? What d'you mean?"

"Usually you won't hear a word said against him."

"That's from others. Course I won't. People put him down they put us all down. But seeing as there's nobody else here ..." he grinned, looking around at the three hundred or so people lazying around the gardens.

"No, right," Penny replied, looking at Jimmy a little quizzically, her head slightly to one side. "Yeah, well, so where was I ..."

"This girl from over Barking way?"

"Oh yeah," she laughed. "That bump seems to have done me more damage than you!"

"Yeah, well ..." Jimmy began, looking hard into her eyes. "I'm sorry if I worried you. I did hear what you said, about being careful. Then I go and fall off like some granny on roller skates."

"Exactly, clown! But what I was saying? This girl, Mae ..."

"She nice?" Jimmy asked, winking.

"Very. Far too nice for you."

"Oh really. How would Sally understand that remark?"

"That reminds me, I want to talk to you about Sally … But Mae, she says this big, big thing out at Clacton Mikey wants to copy was a total joke. Those flash East End types are taking the piss out of you. There were only four or five bikers there! Versus forty or fifty of them … Wouldn't you skedaddle?"

"With those odds …" he pondered theatrically. "Yep!"

"See."

"Yeah, but there will be far more here Penny. I don't think there's any doubt about that. And regardless of what our illustrious poser says when he comes back, fortune favours the brave. Or as Athene put it: 'it is the bold man who every time does best' …"

"Did she now …"

"Well, no, she actually said something pretty unpronounceable in Greek, but that's what she meant!" Jimmy laughed, a combination of Penny's cheery prettiness and the purple heart making him feel much, much better. Ready, in fact. "And I tell you, those two faces we met up with, Charlie and Jon, they're good guys. So don't worry, we'll be alright. Me, Manny, Keith, Pete, Charlie and Jon, we'll look after each other … you keep Toby out of it mind."

"Too right. No way am I taking him home with a broken nose. And Mikey?"

"I had him and that Stevie down for holding the coats," Jimmy laughed.

"Mmm," Penny giggled mockingly. "Might be a tough ask!"

"You feeling on better form now dude?" Jon asked, sitting to join them.

"Sure, course. I'm sat here with the prettiest girl in town, what's not to feel good about?" Jimmy smiled back.

"You mean that Jimmy Carlton?" Penny asked.

"You seen anyone prettier?" he asked of Jon.

"Nope, not even close," Jon replied, his flirting eyes now capturing Penny's.

"Seems official then," Jimmy suggested, smiling a little half-heartedly on noticing how easily Jon's attention forced Penny into a somewhat shy, girly smile.

"You gonna look after him then?" she asked of Jon, nodding her head towards Jimmy.

"Well," he laughed. "Don't seem we can trust him to look after himself!"

"True that," she nodded.

"Then again, some cats just have the full nine … or in Jimmy's case, nine minus one but that should be enough for today. So don't worry, he'll be OK."

"You believe in destiny then?" Penny asked.

"Believe? I'm not sure I'd go so far as *believe*. I mean, I think I could make something of my life, be something. But the key is in the making not the wishing, don't you think?"

"Oh no, not another grammar school boy!"

"Yeah, why, what's the problem?" he asked, the wind suddenly quiet in his sails.

"The problem is I can't understand half of what this one says," she smiled sweetly, flicking her thumb towards Jimmy.

"Don't listen," Jimmy said. "She's smart enough."

"Me," Penny laughed. "I'm just a typist. What do I know?"

"That's what you do Penny. It isn't what you are," Jon suggested.

She looked at him for a moment. Looked into his big, dark eyes trying to decide whether she thought he was winding her up, chatting her up or simply being nice. He was a good looking guy, no doubt about that. But there was something else about him. A kind of certainty in those eyes that was really quite warming, reassuring.

"So what are you going to make of your life?" she asked.

"Hmm," Jon smiled, nodding as if to say touché. "Guess I've set myself up here. OK, well truth is I'm not that sure. I'm working in this advertising agency. I like it, seems I'm good at some of it."

"Such as?"

"It's … it's not that easy to explain. Mostly, at the moment, I get the job of finding the right location or music or whatever to make the mood. But I'm getting to write stuff too …"

"OK …"

"Yeah … But a couple of the guys there, they're like four or five years older than me and … Well, lately they've been talking about moving on, getting into making films. I think that's what I'd really like to do. So I guess I'm going to hang along with them. See where it goes."

"Wow, yeah," Penny nodded, impressed. "That sounds cool. You think that sounds cool Jimmy?"

"Nah man," Jimmy smiled back. "You'd be better off in a bank. Pay's good, hours aren't bad. Good, safe, steady job in the bank …" he continued, his voice slowing and lowering with every syllable till finally he pretended to fall asleep in mid-sentence.

"Sad, isn't it?" Penny smiled to Jon. "Jealousy."

"Pitiful," he agreed.

"So is that your destiny you think?" she asked of Jimmy. "A career in the bank?"

"Who knows," Jimmy shrugged.

"Well Jon here seems to think we can be whatever we put our mind to being. You not think that?"

"Well, if you want a serious answer. No."

"Why not?"

"Stuff. Shit happens. You make great plans then a wheel falls off ..."

"Or you fall off your wheels," Jon laughed with a kindly smile in his eyes.

"Well, yeah," Jimmy nodded, accepting the jibe. "I was thinking about this earlier, sitting on Keith's scooter feeling sorry for myself, cursing my luck ..."

"So falling off acting the fool was bad luck, yeah?" Penny challenged.

"No. No, I can't say that can I," he smiled self-critically. "And up to a point I'd agree with Jon about making good things happen. I think you can manage your luck well or you can manage it badly."

"But you're still saying luck's around, things happen by chance?" Jon asked.

"Well, yes. You ever read Boethius?"

"Er, yeah ..." Jon pondered. "Yeah, I think we did."

"Not more greek stuff," Penny sighed.

"Roman," Jimmy smiled. "His idea was this. Everyone's born with good luck and bad. We've each got a jar of each. Now he says yes, if you manage your luck well you might get to waste the bad where it doesn't matter and save the good for when it does. But not always. Sometimes it's just out of your control."

"Well?" Penny asked smilingly of Jon, like she was the dealer in a game of poker.

"Why? Why is it sometimes possible to control it, other times not?"

"Lady Fortune. She's the problem."

"But surely, she's just a convenient myth. Someone to blame on those days when you get up too careless to make your own luck?"

"Hmm, well, put like that …" Jimmy smiled, nodding respectfully.

"So is that it?" Penny asked after a moment. "You give in?"

"No," Jimmy smiled. "I was thinking. You read the horoscopes, don't you. In the Standard and that?"

"Yeah, sometimes," Penny nodded.

"What for?"

"See what's going to happen!" she giggled.

"But you don't really believe in them, right?"

"No, of course not. It's just a bit of fun."

"I agree. But it's useful fun, isn't it? You read something that says some glamorous actress got this great part because Jupiter had the hots for Mars or whatever and you think: so that's why they didn't pick me."

"Yeah, exactly," Penny smiled.

"OK," Jon nodded. "But that's more or less the same as your point about Lady Fortune. Belief in the stars and fate saves people beating themselves up with lots of 'why not me' questions. That what you're saying?"

"I guess. But I think there's another point. I'm not saying making films wouldn't be great. I also think you'd be good at it and I wouldn't. But Penny here is gooey about film-makers, less so about those that look after their money."

"Gooey?" she asked, head to one side.

"You know what I mean. The problem is, people being what they are, they can't help but glamorise some things - some jobs, some places, some people. But to balance things out, if you glamorise some ideas you put down others. So being rich is better than being poor, being pretty better than being ugly."

"Well it is, isn't it?" Penny asked.

"Yes, if you happen to be pretty," Jimmy smiled. "But what about all those poor, ugly women. How they get through the day?"

"Hmm, that's clever," Jon nodded. "But it still doesn't disprove my point. Yes, some people are born ugly. That's tough ... and maybe it gets in the way. I mean, no-one's going to get the job of receptionist at our place with mangy hair, face like the back of an elephant and breath like a sewer. But she'd do OK on the phones ..."

"You know as well as I do that she wouldn't get that job either," Jimmy argued.

"No. OK. But she might somewhere else. But anyway," Jon hurried along. "I'm saying yeah, if you want, let's think of fate like you're thinking of luck. There are lots of good possibilities, lots of bad ones. I still think the sharpest people will always get most of the good things - jobs, friends, the lot."

"Yeah," Penny put in sceptically. "But why? That's Jimmy's question. Is it because they deserve it? I mean, sometimes shit happens to really nice people while total arses get rich."

"But that *is* my point," Jon insisted. "Shit doesn't happen to nice people *because* they're nice, it happens despite that. It happens because for all their niceness they make too few right choices, too many bad ones. I just don't think that some things are meant to be."

"So what are they?"

"They are made to be. Sure, beauty's good to have ... if you've got it," he suggested, catching Penny's eye with the glint in his own. "But take the Rolling Stones. Those are five seriously ugly cats, but they'll make it bigger than a pretty boy band like the Small Faces because they want it more."

"So you don't get what you deserve, you get what you want. Is that it?"

"No. No I'm not saying you get what you want as though wanting is all you have to do. Wanting isn't enough. But at the same time, deserve is just wishful thinking. I'm saying you get what you make happen."

"Well?" Penny mused, looking to Jimmy.

"I accept that up to a point. Yes, it's OK to say that right thinking people get out there and try to make good things happen, while duffers are those that sit around moaning because the world's not beating a path to their door …"

"But?"

"But then some lazy, half-sozzled prat wins the pools!"

"Hmm, yeah …" Jon pondered.

"But then maybe …" Penny began. "Maybe we're looking at the wrong part of the story …"

"Go on," Jon encouraged.

"Well, so you were both saying things like wealth and fame and beauty don't always go to those that would use them well. Meaning we shouldn't judge people a success of failure by whether or not they've got them. Right?"

"Right," Jon and Jimmy agreed.

"But what about judging by how they use them?"

"Hmm," Jon nodded, thoughtful and full of respect, adding for Jimmy: "Like you said …"

"More than smart enough," Jimmy completed the thought.

"I am still here you know!"

"You are, and you are right," Jimmy smiled.

"Oh, right, well … wow," Penny cooed, fully chuffed with herself.

"If at heart you are one complete tosser," he continued, "then becoming rich or famous won't change you. On the other hand, if your character is good then success won't make you an arse."

"But earlier you said you can't stop people glamorising fame and beauty …"

"And film making!" Jon put in lightly.

"Exactly!" Penny laughed.

"But in the end," he suggested with renewed seriousness. "We mustn't let ourselves be distracted or upset by the opinions of people who really don't matter to us."

"That's right," Jimmy insisted. "Sure, I might get the hump with people who think I'm some kind of cardigan wearing Mr Average for working in a bank. But you have to look past that. It's what those you care about think that really matters."

"I agree," Jon nodded.

"So long as they don't think you're a loser, then life is good," Jimmy smiled to Penny, looking into her eyes with greater intensity and affection than he had ever previously allowed himself.

"Well," Penny began. "I can't say I'm over the moon about you getting into this fight. Either of you for that matter," she continued, looking to Jon and then back to Jimmy. "But I guess that just says I care?"

"I promise I'll bring him back in one piece," Jimmy said, nodding to Jon.

"Same," Jon smiled.

Chapter 4

So come on, I wanna see you baby
Come on, I don't mean maybe
Come on, I'm tryin' to make you see
That I belong to you and you belong to me
Come on.

Come On
Chuck Berry

"Come on," Pete had called. "We're supposed to go and listen."

Jimmy and Jon did as they were told, leaving Penny to smile ruefully on the foolishness of boys.

By the time they got to the portico it was as good as over. But according to Manny they hadn't missed much. Some local face, guy calling himself King Al - which meant he had to be a pillock as far as Manny was concerned - said they thought there were three groups of bikers down on the seafront. So, it had been agreed - he'd evidently said all pompous, like he and the few other self-appointed chiefs were some kind of War Council - that they would also split into three.

All of which added up to this: the west London cats together with locals from Crawley and Brighton would take the crowd parked up along Marine Parade; the East End and Medway boys would hit the group lounging up on the Aquarium Sun Terrace; the south Londoners with the few from Surrey would take the mob on the Palace Pier.

So, they rode. Heading out east for a few blocks along Edward Street then down Bedford Street to the front. There must have been at least 250 scooters now, every one of which meant something important to its owner. Made a statement about them.

Sat on the back of Keith's TV, Jimmy felt quite proud really. Sure, he wished he'd been on his own scooter - you had to be taken for a bit of a loser riding passenger. But when all was said and done, Keith's was the better machine. By far. And with a second heart now clearing his mind he felt good once again. Confident, calm and full of certain conviction.

He understood Penny's point about Boy's Own macho crap. She was right, of course - if you insist on seeing things in proportion with all that grown up rational reasonableness girls seem to learn so easily. But there was no point getting old before your time. If you can't fuck about when you're young when you ever going to?

As they cruised along Marine Parade he saw all the bikes. He knew the names of some of them, not many but it was worth knowing a little about your rivals. He spotted an old BSA A7, several Triumphs and Nortons, an Ariel and a Triton. The guys hanging around them all seemed, compared to his people, much older. Maybe it was the clothes - leather or waxed jackets, greasy jeans - but they all seemed kind of worn out, unhealthy like. Oh well, that's their look out.

He gave a bit of verbal as they drove past a jeering crowd and then sat back, taking a few deep breaths. He knew Brighton well enough. Knew where they were going to park up on Castle Square. Knew the route down from there. They were close, not long now.

There was excitement and tension in the air as they left the scooters and walked back down through the Lanes to Grand Junction Road. About fifty yards short of the pier they stopped, they and the Rockers all taunting and laughing at each other.

There were about seventy of them, mostly decent sized guys. A few with chains. Most with bits of broken deck chair held like a baseball bat. They also had a fair sized fire burning, fuelled by broken deck chairs and some planking they'd obviously ripped from a rundown ice cream kiosk by the railings.

"Wankers," Mikey had shouted from a few ranks behind Jimmy.

Exactly as he'd planned, exactly as he'd assured Penny - who was safe at the back with Dawn and Toby - he was in a tight group with Manny, Keith, Pete, Charlie and Jon. Also with them near the front were a few other top faces they'd met from time to time, place to place. Four from Catford and their two mates from Forest Hill. Four more from Deptford. A couple from Bexley and their cousins from over Hayes way. That was enough. You didn't want to get into a fight with loads of dudes only to find half of them were hoping you'd do all the work.

"OK, let's get this done," Manny had said. He was never a loud or forceful guy, but when a cat that big says it's time to go, it's time to go. Walking slowly to begin with, Manny, Jimmy and the crowd ignored the shouting and the obscenities. Ignored also the hail of small stones. There'd be worse.

Then, as the Rocker mob started to spread out - those guys also making sure they were with the ones they most trusted - Manny started to walk more quickly. More purposefully.

A group of maybe twenty bikers on their right flank started forward. They were obviously confident guys, staring straight at Manny, like they wanted to say: he's a big guy, we're big bastards too. Accepting the challenge Manny started to run, which was cue enough.

Knowing speed was one of their key weapons, Jimmy, Jon and Pete broke into a sprint, heading towards the middle of the greaser mob who stopped and stood stock still. Ready with chains and staves from broken chairs.

As if they'd trained together, the three of them veered slightly left, heading for the six bikers at the end of their line. Then, just a few yards from engagement, the three of them kicked their heels, missing a step. It wasn't much, but it was enough.

Seeing them that close all six bikers swung - but swung too early, the large and ugly geezer on the very end noticeably so. Having been spinning his chain nonchalantly in a simple wheel he reached back and brought the sharp, broken links around in a wide arc, the tip of which missed Jimmy's face by a couple of feet, easy.

Now he was fucked. With the chain wrapped around the back of his left leg, his right arm fastened across his chest, he could not help but lean over on his left side.

With his fist tightly clasped Jimmy swung and caught pug-faced greaser full between his now scared eyes. The sound of the narrow strip of bone breaking could be heard above the sound of shouting and fighting across to Jimmy's right. Stopping just past his man, Jimmy elbowed him hard near his right kidney. Then, as the guy reached round to where the pain was he chopped the side of his right hand against the back of the guy's neck, kicking him in the stomach as he fell.

Manny, Keith, Pete and Jon were each getting the better of their guys. But, as he looked across, Jimmy saw two large bikers, both with chains, stepping towards Charlie who was already having a tough time with a geezer who was clearly no mug. He knew if he didn't move now his friend would be isolated.

Picking up a piece of broken deck chair Jimmy ran across to Pete's fight, smashing the wooden stave down on the greaser's head. He fell instantly, his face already bloodied from Pete's fists - Jimmy knew no-one who could throw punches more quickly than Pete. "Charlie," he shouted.

Understanding instantly, Pete picked up a chain and another couple of deck chair legs, tossing one to Jimmy. The two of them intercepted the two large greasers, Pete using his chain to snare that   being swung at Charlie's head, Jimmy using his stave to crack the forearm of the other biker before he could swing.

Now it was just fists. Pete and Jimmy both went at it all in, confident their speed and power would win against brawn and size. Charlie too was also starting to win and win well, three heavy hits pounding into his man's belly.

Jimmy looked his guy in the eyes, laughing to himself at the stupid star tattoos on either ear. "Faggot," he sneered while lining the geezer up with a heavy left to the ribs, leaning back slightly to drive a full-power right-handed uppercut into his throat followed by a swinging clump with his left which took the guy full on the side of his mouth. As he fell, his hands hitting the decking Jimmy stamped on his wrist, snapping it easily.

Jimmy, Pete and Charlie stood together for a moment, regathering their breath as they checked on their mates. A couple of the Catford boys were looking groggy and bloodied - Manny was moving them away, out if it.

Over by the boarded-up café Keith and Jon had teamed up with the Deptford cats, the six of them smashing six bikers mercilessly. The cause of their especially vicious anger was obvious: the two Forest Hills guys were slumped against the wall, bleeding badly from knife wounds.

"Let's get them away," Pete called.

Walking calmly through the mayhem Pete, Charlie and Jimmy helped the two young faces to their feet and led them across the pier to catch up with Manny, who was headed towards a small group of youngsters and women watching safely from just below the bus station. Dawn, Toby and Penny amongst them.

"You done then?" Dawn asked of Manny.

"Not yet, just do what you can for these, yeah?" the big guy said, turning without waiting for an unwanted reply.

Jimmy didn't say anything, just helped the Forest Hill boys sit on a bench. He caught Penny's eye for a moment, but really didn't need to linger there. Nothing she was thinking or wanting to say mattered at that moment.

It was Charlie that saw them first. Just as they got back to the fighting a small army of around fifty Police with batons came marching down from the town, flanked by four tall, imposing coppers on four even taller, even more imposing greys.

The bikers saw them too. Saw them and turned. About twenty of them jumped over the railings down onto the beach, running off towards the West Pier.

"Come on," Jimmy shouted, instantly sprinting after the fleeing group. As he sprung back up after landing on the unforgiving pebbles he felt a large stone hit him hard against the left shoulder. "Fuck," he screamed as the pain seared down his arm and across his chest.

Guys were landing all around him now, his mates, the Deptford guys, those posh cousins from Bexley and Hayes, all holding up their forearms to deflect the hail of stones as they ran towards the fleeing rockers.

"Get up you poser!" Jon ordered with an unsympathetic grin as he ran past.

Soon the adrenalin kicked in, mixed itself with the fury still strong in his blood. No way was Jimmy Carlton finishing now. No way indeed was he finishing last. The stiffness replacing the pain would be a handicap, he knew that. But so what, he had another arm, another fist.

Picking himself up he sprinted - as best you can on a pebble beach - passing Manny, Keith and Charlie with ease. But Pete and Jon were still out front, as fast as him, maybe faster. A couple of the Deptford faces were with them, just as fast, just as committed. And those young cats from Bexley, they were ahead also.

Harder Jimmy ran, feeling his heart pounding, his chest gasping for breath, stones still flying around but pain was nothing now. All that mattered was that they ended it on their terms, how they wanted. No-one runs away from a south London face.

Four of the bikers stopped and turned, snarling as viciously as they could, but their eyes betrayed them. Pete, Jon and the Deptford guys just ran straight into them, knocking them to the ground, falling on top of one each, their arms flailing, fists raining down. The Bexley kids caught up with two more, jumping on their backs to pull them down, then getting instantly to their feet, kicking the prone greasers cruelly.

Jimmy ran past, aiming for two large but obviously flagging geezers just a few feet ahead, the fairground jingle of Prince Buster's *Al Capone* in his head: *don't call me scarface*. With an extra effort he caught them, pushed himself between them, his arms out wide, catching them across the back of the neck before pulling his hands round, gripping them tight, choking them as he pulled them to the ground. The pain in his left arm was excruciating, but so what.

As the guy on his right went to kneel up Jimmy gripped him by his oily hair and rammed his face into the rocky beach. Jumping up he kicked the other guy in the stomach before swinging his foot back to catch the first one on the chin with his heel.

The rest of his crew ran past, falling on the remaining greasers, kicking and punching till the job was done.

Having dusted themselves down, straightened out their gear, checked themselves for damage, they found some steps back up onto King's Road.

Back down by the Palace Pier and the Aquarium it was mayhem still, only now the greasers had all gone. Now it was all those East End and Medway crazies fighting with the Police.

"Oh no," Manny sighed. "That's stupid, that's not what we're here for ..."

"Where's the glory in that?" Jimmy asked rhetorically.

"There is none," Jon replied all the same.

"They are going to be seriously pissed though, the Police. They'll have it in for all of us now," Keith reasoned.

"We need to get out of here," one of the Hayes kids suggested.

"Yeah, you're right," Jimmy nodded. "Head into the town, it'll be quieter there. We just need to catch up with some others then we'll join you, find a club, OK?"

With handshakes and backslaps the group split.

"So what do we do, go down there and find them?" Charlie asked, looking along the seafront. "Shit," he gasped as they watched two of the horses charge at a group of East Enders, who ran back onto the pier. Then, armed with biker chains and broken deck chairs, they suddenly turned, ran back, charging at the Police, taking them by surprise, driving them up towards the bus station now.

"What you reckon?" Keith asked, looking from Manny to Jimmy and back.

"Well, they're not stupid, neither of them. Plus Penny's looking out for her brother so she will have wanted to get away double quick," Manny thought.

"Agree," Jimmy nodded. "Penny will have got them well away from there by now. Headed up into the town."

"And what about those other mates of yours, the chief dude," Jon asked, rolling his eyes with obvious sarcasm.

"Oh yeah," Manny laughed. "Forgot about them! Anyone see anything of Mikey and that Stevie?"

"Nope," Pete replied, rolling his eyes also.

"Guess they're with the girls," Charlie laughed.

"Jimmy?" Manny asked, a playful grin on his face.

"Don't ask me?" Jimmy smiled in reply. "My guess is Charlie's right. Mikey may be a mate but he's no hero."

"But ..." Jon put in, a puzzled look on his face. "Didn't I hear you and that girl of his calling him Odysseus?"

"Maybe ..." Jimmy smiled.

"Well, why?"

"What's Mikey's name Manny?" Jimmy asked.

"O'Dea," Manny replied deadpan.

"Geddit?" Jimmy laughed.

"Oh right, I see," Jon laughed.

"Anyway, worry not," Pete grinned. "His Leaderness is safe. That's them coming down Middle Street."

"Well I'll be ..." Manny sighed quietly, seeing Mikey walking along like he owned the place. Unhurt and unaffected.

At least Stevie Dolan had the decency to look a little sheepish. Maybe he was wrong, but whilst he knew Penny didn't like the fighting Jimmy could have sworn she looked embarrassed too. Hanging back to walk with Dawn and Toby.

"Hi guys," Mikey smiled.

"Well what d'you know," Jon put in, looking disdainfully at the crisp, pristine neatness of Mikey's suit. His oxblood loafers unmarked. His shirt un-dirtied. His short hair neatly combed. "Dudes just run from you?"

"Sorry, what you say?" Mikey asked. He stood strong, trying to look unbothered, but his eyes betrayed a lack of sureness.

He didn't know Jon. Didn't even really know of him. Knew only that the way he looked and the way he dressed meant he was no clown. More than that, the small gash on his right cheek and bruising to the side of his mouth said he'd been the real deal. As did the fact that his longish dark hair was matted and tousled, his seven guinea shoes scuffed, the left knee was out of his houndstooth strides and a couple of buttons were missing from his Austin's shirt.

"I said, we didn't see you," Jon smiled, disrespect obvious in his voice.

"Guess you moved too quick for us," Charlie put in.

"You two trying to vex me?" Mikey asked haughtily.

"Nah, just trying to work you out," Charlie replied, unhurriedly tucking his slightly ripped shirt back into his trousers. "Not a scratch," he added, staring at Mikey accusingly before making some play of straightening out the bent and bleeding fingers of his left hand.

"All OK then Manny?" Mikey asked, trying to ignore Jon and Charlie now.

"Grand," Manny smiled back, carelessly poking a finger into the ripped shoulder of his red Harrington. "You?"

"Yeah, OK. Didn't see much where I was," Mikey suggested just a little too quickly.

"And where was that then Mikey?" Jimmy asked, the pain in his left shoulder making him wince as he tried to feel how much damage had been done to the side seam of his suit jacket. His shirt was finished, he knew that much. Too much blood splattered down the front. Jacket, strides and shirt - he was so glad he hadn't worn the faux-Brioni and white Austin's.

"With you guys … till we got split. Then me and Stevie made it round the back …"

"Those Forest Hill guys OK?" Jimmy asked of Penny, Dawn and Toby, ignoring Mikey now.

"I think so …" Dawn began.

"Sis gave 'em her socks," Toby said proudly.

"What, their feet cold or something?" Jimmy asked, his brow furrowed in puzzlement while looking down to check. Indeed, Penny was no longer wearing those white socks.

"To use as swabs Dumbo," she sneered, a playful glint clear in her eyes.

"Oh yeah, of course. Sorry!" he smiled, acknowledging his dimness. "That was smart, thanks."

"There was a bit of blood, but they didn't think the wounds were too deep. They'll be OK, I'm sure."

"Yeah, thanks ..."

"And the Catford boys?" Manny asked of Dawn.

"They were fine. Came round in a few minutes. Went back to join their mates. You not see them again?"

"No, they didn't come down the beach with us," Manny recalled before suggesting: "But I saw another crowd of greasers running away up West Street, maybe they went for them."

"Round the back of what?" Jon asked after waiting calmly to check Jimmy and Manny were content with their updates.

"Er, round the back ..." Mikey began, before changing tack unconvincingly: "I mean, first off there was a little action further down the pier ..."

"Oh yeah," Pete nodded deadpan. "I saw all those gulls flapping away. Mean creatures ..."

"Then we went round the back of the Aquarium and met up with ..." Mikey continued quickly.

"Remind me," Jon said to Jimmy. "What they call Odysseus?"

"Sacker of cities."

"Sacker of cities, that was it," he smirked. "Hardly know the difference, would you - sacker of cities, scarer of gulls!" he laughed, looking dismissively at Mikey for a moment before turning away with Charlie and Pete, who were both laughing sarcastically also.

"Now hold on ..." Mikey started to bluster.

"Mikey," Jimmy suggested. "Sometimes, when you've got fuck all to say the best thing to do is shut the fuck up."

"What, what you ..." Mikey burst, trying one last time to reclaim respect. Failing.

"Come on, let's go get a coffee or something while the boys get cleaned up," Penny suggested, ending the conversation in a way that, unintentionally no doubt, merely added to Mikey's belittlement. "You coming Dawn?"

"Er, I guess," Dawn replied while looking pleadingly at Manny.

"Well," the big guy began, thinking. In the end, he knew he had no choice. It would be too shitty to make Dawn go on her own. Whilst at the same time he knew having her around would inhibit the guys talking about their afternoon. "OK. What you gonna do?" he asked of Jimmy.

"Well, guess we'll do as Penny says. Get straight, check how the other faces are doing. Then we'll all be ready for a club, don't you think?"

"Oh yeah," Pete put in. "Local cat said to me, before it all went off, that the best blues club is called The Barn - want to try for that?"

"OK, where is it?"

"Guy said in West Street. That's just kind of over there, I think," Pete said, pointing diagonally across the sea front buildings.

"Alright, we'll find it."

"Penny," Toby began a little timidly.

"Jimmy?" she replied instantly.

"Sure, of course, we'll look after him. It's quieting down now."

"OK, but if they get into any more bother," Penny warned her brother. "You keep out."

"Don't worry," Pete smiled. "We're done scaring sea gulls!"

Jimmy did feel a pang of guilt as he watched Mikey turn away. But that was all. A small pang, no more. Added up on the great abacus of life, he really didn't give a toss how or where his mate had run to.

At the same time, he understood Jon's point. If you're a coward you are best off keeping out of it. Not only are you of no use to yourself, there's a danger you'll just get in other people's way.

But it was more than just that. Mikey had become a coward wrapped up in bullshit.

That wasn't cool.

That simply could not be allowed to pass.

His mum had been right, totally. No way was the loser anything like good enough for Penny.

Then again, unless he was reading it all wrong, just now Penny's face seemed to say she'd just realised that too.

Chapter 5

There is a house in New Orleans
They call the Rising Sun
And it's been the ruin of many a poor boy
And God I know I'm one.

House Of The Rising Sun
The Animals

The guys worked their way through a few backstreets to a spot just above the bus station. The fighting between the Police and East Enders was almost over, and whist there were a few angry looking coppers wandering around, most seemed to see the difference between the people heading back into the town and the crew they'd now got pretty much penned-in on the pier.

A couple of large wagons flew down West Street. Clearly, there were going to be arrests and, Jimmy had no doubt, a great deal of paper talk 'about how the young people of today seemed to lack respect for the country their parents had sacrificed so much to save' … and so on.

They met up with a few groups they knew as they followed the general drift up into the town. A few spoke of guys that had taken a bit of a beating, but nothing major - on either side. A couple of local cats talked up a Turkish coffee shop on Churchill Square where they could chill out for a while, wait for the Police to calm down.

The owner of the Istanbul was a big, cheery dude called Mustafa. He seemed genuinely unaware of what had been happening down on the front, which was probably just as well. His coffee was just the best. Rich and dark, with which they all took the house special: a cup cake topped with thick, sweet chocolate icing.

Despite the sugar injection, Jimmy was feeling groggy again. The pain in his left shoulder, where the stone had hit, was so merged in with the various pains from the accident that he just felt numb all down that side. Indeed, even the left side of his head felt numb. He no longer had a headache as such, more a constant sense of a kind of dizzying humming. His eyes too felt tired, his lids heavy, his vision a little blurred.

Sure, he smiled and nodded as the guys chatted about the fighting. And he managed to join in as his table and most of the others started to sing along with John Lee Hooker belting out *I'm A Man* from the jukebox. But overall, he was not exactly at his best. A long way from it, if truth will out.

All told, there were now about fifty guys in there. All cheery and happy. A bit loud maybe, but Mustafa didn't seem to mind. On the contrary really seeing as he was singing along also. The two girls that worked the Gaggia - and generally seemed to do all the rest of the work - just smiled on indulgently.

"You reckon they fuck?" Toby asked Jimmy, trying to sound hard and cool but succeeding only in sounding silly. A schoolboy thinking a rude word makes him a man.

"Oh yeah, sure of it," Jimmy nodded. "With their boyfriends. You see those two six foot four Turks out the back?"

"What? Where?" Toby asked, like he was really worried.

"You still looking to get laid Toby boy?" Pete asked.

"What, me … yeah, sure. When I want to like …" the boy tried to suggest with nonchalance.

"OK, fine," Pete nodded. "If you're all sorted, that's fine. You can wait outside …"

"Sorry?"

"Wait outside Cilla's - we won't be long."

"Bit of a dump, isn't it?" Jimmy asked.

"Yeah," Pete grinned. "And the problem with that is?"

"Nothing I guess. They still have that Friday night clinic down at the Dreadnought?"

"I really wouldn't know," Pete laughed before turning to Keith. "Jimmy boy's just asked if someone could drop him down at some clinic at the Dreadnought, any idea?"

"Nah," Keith shook his head, before adding: "Oh yeah, now you mention it I did hear a cat some weeks back talking about a clap clinic. Think he did call it something like that ... down in Greenwich, that right Jimmy?" he asked.

"Ho hum," Jimmy smiled thinly. At least the dizziness in his head was easing.

"Wh-what is Cilla's?" Toby asked.

"It's a brothel kid," Charlie explained, before rejoining John Lee: "Man, spells M A N ..."

"You going?" the boy asked Jimmy.

"Me?" Jimmy laughed. "No kid. Apart from the fact I doubt I could keep it up ..."

"I'd heard that," Pete nodded sympathetically. "Sally's been telling I'm afraid."

"As I was saying," Jimmy continued, ignoring his friend. "Apart from the fact my left side is a numb as a whore's fanny, some of us can get it without paying," he finished, smirking dismissively at Pete.

"Get what you pay for in this world," Pete countered. "Quality costs. Look at Jon's shirt ... no, forget that ..." he suggested seeing the torn fabric where buttons once were.

"You want to take him?" Jimmy asked.

"You think it'll be alright, with Penny I mean?"

"I think it would very much not be alright with Penny," Jimmy replied. "You going Keith?"

"Nah, did alright last night."

"That redhead?"

"Yeah," the guy smiled with a mixture of pride and shyness.

"Cute chick. How about you two?"

"Well, to tell you the truth," Charlie replied. "Yeah. I haven't had a good fuck in weeks."

"Does 'good' mean 'any' in that sentence?" Jon asked.

"Maybe," Charlie considered good-naturedly.

"That should be OK, don't you think?" Jon asked of Jimmy.

"You not interested?""

"No. I agree with you. Paying's for losers. But seeing as we've got a prize pair right here with us, might as well let the kid have some fun. Don't you think?"

"We do this for you," Jimmy began, looking sternly at Toby, "and then find out you've told your sister, we cut off your balls. You understand?"

"I won't tell her Jimmy, course I won't."

"With blunt scissors," Jimmy added menacingly before turning to Pete and Charlie. "You cool with looking after him?"

"Seriously Jimmy, we're hardly going to let anything happen. Penny'd kill us!" Pete laughed a little nervously, knowing the truth of what he'd just said.

"Exactly!" Jimmy nodded. "Alright. Maybe we'll get another coffee and then come along and sit outside."

Jon came back after a few minutes with three fresh mugs. As he sat he pulled a twenty pack of Number 6 from one pocket, a small brown paper bag from another.

"Good stuff," he smiled, nodding to the bag. "Jamaican dude on Railton Road gets it. Sells it in The George."

Jimmy and Keith watched in some admiration as Jon carefully and methodically pulled the leaves off a fat bud and dropped them into a saucer, picking out the hard stalks. Then, with two spoons he slowly ground the weed until the green stuff was fine and evenly spread. Next, he emptied the tobacco from a couple of Number 6 and mixed it with the marijuana. Last, having gummed four Rizla reds together, he made a roach from a part of the cigarette packet and, with calm precision, rolled the thing into a slim cone, twisting the paper at the fat end to hold it all tight.

No-one in the café batted an eyelid.

"So," Jon said, finishing his coffee, looking across the cup to Jimmy and Keith. "Guess I'll have to apologise to your mate?"

"Whatever for?" Keith asked.

"Giving him a hard time over the fighting."

"You will do no such thing," Keith replied.

"Don't you think I embarrassed him a bit? You know, in front of his girl and all."

"Well sure, but so what?" Jimmy put in.

"Yeah, well, I didn't think you'd mind!" Jon laughed, starting to make a second spliff.

"What you mean by that?"

"I mean, you have obviously got a big thing for her. Making him look bad gives you a better chance."

"Honestly," Jimmy began, a little put out. "I never …"

"It's OK," Jon smiled. "I'm not saying you've ratted on him. On the contrary, you've probably stood up for him when he hasn't deserved it."

"Yep," Keith nodded.

"You too?" Jimmy asked.

"Me too what? I'm just agreeing with Jon. You always do stand up for Mikey O'Dea, even when he doesn't deserve it … which is most of the fucking time."

"See," Jon said, nodding towards Keith for emphasis while looking straight at Jimmy. "Just like Athene."

"Sorry?" Keith asked.

"Athene," Jimmy repeated. "She was the goddess who favoured Odysseus, regardless of how big a fool he acted or how many of his men he led to a grisly death."

"Yeah, well," he sighed with a mix of disinterest and incomprehension.

"Well, you did ask!" Jon laughed, twisting the second reefer into shape. "You guys ready?"

"You got another of those?" Keith asked.

"I have," Jon nodded. "As if I'd make the two of you share!"

"I reckon the park opposite Cilla's will do fine," Jimmy suggested.

The three of them sat on a wide, slatted wooden bench on the south side of Clifton Gardens, enjoying the early evening sea breeze, the late summer sun and the smell and taste of good weed.

"Yeah man," Keith sighed slowly, appreciatively and slightly giggly whilst breathing out a long plume of grey smoke. "Well nice stuff. Well nice.'

"Told you," Jon smiled.

"You know, I was thinking …"

"Steady on Keith, you're a mechanic for fuck's sake," Jimmy laughed while holding on to a deep drag from his reefer.

"Oh yeah …" Keith smiled good-naturedly. "About your scooter. I reckon I could fit TV panels. Might need a bit of fiddling, but if I could find a pair we could chrome them up a bit. Give the thing more shape and style ... you reckon?"

"Yeah ..." Jimmy began a little pensively. "I mean, if you think ..."

"Yeah, well, guess I need to look to the front end first. You've mangled that totally," Keith smiled ruefully.

"You think it all worth it?" Jon asked Jimmy. "I mean, your man may fix it perfect, but would you ever feel right on it? Your trust in things gets damaged when they let you down, don't you think?"

"Yeah, well, think I let the bike down really," Jimmy suggested, shaking his head slowly while taking a long pull on his spliff. "But maybe all of that's a lesson. Maybe I should think of getting a car or something ..."

"A car?" Keith burst almost splenetically. "You poser!"

"Yeah, well, it's just an idea ..." Jimmy apologised.

"I think you're right though," Jon suggested. "I mean, OK, my scooter's crap anyway so who am I to speak ..."

"I might be getting hold of a '58 LD150 if you're interested," Keith smiled. "Needs some work but I'll do it for cost. Might add a pair of chromed-up TV panels if you fancy ..."

"Really," Jon smiled. "Well, I suppose, if the price is right and all that."

"Pfff! You're about as constant as Odysseus. Sell your mates for a chance with Calypso!"

"Mates?" Jon asked, wrinkling his nose while looking to Keith. "Any idea what he's on about?"

"Not usually!" Keith laughed. "You guys serious?" he continued after a while. "About cars I mean."

"Well, yeah," Jon replied. "I mean, OK, scooters have been a thing for us all. But soon enough everyone will have a car. That's the future."

"Sure, I know you're right. Nothing lasts forever."

"I don't think that's true Keith," Jimmy suggested seriously. "I mean, friendships, good times, those things must mean more than which Lambretta you ride …"

"Or fall off?"

"Exactly!"

"I've got my eyes on a Mini," Jon put in. "Belongs to this posh chick I know, she's thinking of selling it."

"Yeah, I like those too," Jimmy nodded. "Cool."

"Nah, give me Charlie's battered old Bedford truck any day," Keith grinned. "I will say this though, things are changing. I mean, this, today. It's all been good fun and that, but at the same time …" he mused, falling silent a second. "Well, for a start, all that shit with those idiots from the East End."

"I agree," Jimmy nodded. "My dad's going to say something and I really don't know how I'm going to reply. I mean, I don't think there's anything wrong with two bunches of guys slugging it out for a while. But that was just between us. Start in on the Police and next thing you know the paper's will be full of 'end of the world as we know it' bullshit."

"Yeah," Jon agreed. "And 'is this what we fought for?' head-shaking."

"Your dad fight?" Jimmy asked.

"Yeah. Got captured too. Came home in a right state evidently."

"Keith's dad didn't come back," Jimmy explained sadly.

"Did manage to get home a couple of times. Least, that's how my mum accounts for me and my sister!" Keith smiled thinly. "Then got killed in '44."

"Mikey's dad was a spiv," Jimmy put in.

"Why am I not surprised," Jon laughed while patting Keith with a consoling fist on the shoulder.

"Funnily enough, he got a mention over breakfast."

"Who did?" Keith asked.

"Paddy O'Dea. Well, my mum doesn't much like him or Mikey. Anyway, so my dad's being generous like, saying it's not Mikey's fault his dad was no good. Then, when he gets on to me about coming down here he says something like: don't put no trust in that boy, bravery and looking out for others, those things is hereditary."

"Smart man, your father," Keith nodded.

"Maybe," Jimmy thought. "I mean, you don't really know, do you. I've had my run-ins with him. But I do see he's a decent bloke. Stands square against what he thinks is wrong and all that. But ..."

"Now's another time," Jon suggested. "That's the truth of it. I mean, we can't really know what it was like for them, you know, during the war and that."

"Different to previous wars I guess though, don't you?" Keith offered.

"Well, yeah, actually I do think that," Jon nodded. "I mean, I always got so bored hearing about it when I was a kid. But you go back in history and the people at home didn't really know what the fuck was going on. This time, it came to them."

"I guess," Keith pondered. "Course, my mum never spoke about it much when I was a kid. I didn't get it at the time, but I also see now how people avoided the subject for fear of upsetting her. You know, not wanting to remind her of Albert."

"That your dad?"

"Yeah. Course, I don't have any memory of him at all. I was two and something when he was killed, but I don't think I saw him for more than a few weeks in that time. My sister thinks she has some memories, but ... well, I guess the point is, she'd like to have them. Me too, but they're not there and that's it."

The three of them pondered their thoughts for a moment, taking comfort in the dying embers of their reefers while staring lightheadedly into the redness that shimmered from behind the houses on the west side of the square.

"Like you said," Jimmy thought, looking at Jon, his face pursed with a touch of melancholy. "It's a different time now. I think my old man knows that. I'm not sure he fully gets it, but he's not like completely against everything."

"Mine's always on about the blacks," Jon allowed. "Them and all the pig-ugly flats that are going up in place of some department store on Battersea Park Road."

"Really? Shit, my mum would definitely have lost it if the Germans had bombed Jones and Higgins!"

"Oh, this wasn't the Germans. It's all down to those 'socialist ponces' according to my dad. Not that he seems too sure who they actually are. Then again, he's not usually too fussed about facts!"

"Things are going to carry on changing, though," Keith suggested, stamping out his dead spliff. "And not all for the worse by any chalk. I mean, look at you two."

"Us?"

"Yeah. You're obviously both clever. Well, guys were clever before you, but they still ended up in factories or down mines …"

"Or fixing banged-up scooters!" Jimmy smiled.

"Yeah. Well, kind of. The way I see it, there will always be a need for guys making and fixing things like me and Pete - and no doubt fancy sparkies like Mikey. But nowadays, kids from our kind of background can get to be something else if they want, don't you think?"

"I reckon my sister'll become a teacher," Jimmy said. "Go off to university and all that."

"She good-looking?" Jon asked.

"Well, you're not going to believe this, only knowing her brother," Keith smiled. "But yeah! Very, as it happens."

"Hands off, she's only fifteen."

"Fifteen? Perfect! Young girls are always so grateful!" Jon grinned lasciviously.

"Yeah, well this one has a mother that could break your balls with one slap," Jimmy warned.

"Ouch," Jon gasped laughingly. "My kid brother, Mark, he's bright too. But his big thing is playing guitar. Been at it for a couple of years now. Got a band at school. They're good, I tell you."

"I saw that Clapton a couple of months back," Keith noted.

"Yeah? He as good as they say?"

"Well, I'm not really the one to ask, but he seemed pretty good to me. Not sure about the rest of the band, all look like hairdressers! Not him though, deadly serious all the way through. Nice guitar, sort of red and amber, like a sunset ..."

"Well, if it looks cool it must be good!" Jon laughed.

"Gibson, I think. They're meant to be the best, aren't they?"

"So they say. That's certainly what our Mark wants. I said I'd try and get him one. Keep meaning to take a look down Denmark Street ... Aristotle would approve."

"Eh?" Keith replied blankly.

"Aristotle," Jimmy explained. "Another old greek guy. He said the best flute should always be played by the best flute player."

"Eh?" Keith said again, a wrinkled up look of incomprehension all over his face. "Don't you mean guys that can really play go out and get themselves a good guitar or whatever?"

"Sure, obviously you'd expect someone as good as this cat Clapton to have a classy guitar, not some piece of plastic crap from Woolworth's. But think about things from the guitar's point of view."

"What?"

"What's the point being this fantastically well-made and super-cool looking thing if, instead of getting Eric, you end up going to some rich haddock with five thumbs on both hands?"

"That would not be right as far as Aristotle's concerned," Jon suggested. "Yet, we all know that in the real world, if you've got the money you can get what you want. No shop's gonna say: sorry mate, come back when you've learned a few more chords."

"Well, exactly," a still uncertain Keith replied.

"But Aristotle's saying: hold on, shouldn't we care whether someone is actually good enough to have the best of things? Whether they deserve them?"

"But, I mean, like you said, you can't stop a rich kid buying a Gibson."

"No, and Aristotle knows that. He only uses the flute thing to make the point easy to understand. But what he's really wanting us to think about is the way in which we pick people out. The way we praise them and respect them. Honour them. He says the best of people - those with with the best character, those with virtue and quality - they should get the best of things …"

"OK …"

"And to emphasise the point he puts it the other way round. The best of things, he says, don't deserve to be left in the hands of prats just because they happen to be rich or a Lord or whatever."

"Oh, right. Bit of a socialist then was he, this Aristotle?" Keith laughed.

"Well, no, not really," Jon smiled. "I mean, he was from a wealthy family, didn't need to work. But more than any of that, he absolutely did not think people were equal. Meaning he didn't hold with everyone being treated the same."

"Quite the opposite," Jimmy continued. "What worried him was that there were a lot of newly rich dudes around at the time, flashing the cash. He wanted people to see that it wasn't wealth that made people important, it was the way they acted. The things they did for others. Those who acted best were the best of people, worthy of respect because they earned it."

"That's got something, I think," Jon concluded. "We need to take care to earn and deserve respect. Do the right thing whenever we can, not the easy thing. That's what he's saying."

"Right, yeah," Keith nodded. "Like I said, I never really met my dad, but I cannot but respect the guy. He did what had to be done, like your dad, like Jimmy's."

"It's still a fuck up he didn't come back though," Jon smiled, giving Keith another consoling pat.

"Of course. You know, I do wonder at times though whether things weren't simpler for them. I mean, I don't know what your father does, but mine worked the barges. His two brothers still do, like my grandfather and his brothers before them. War breaks out, off they go, like their father and uncles did before them. I'm not saying it was better, just simpler."

"I get that," Jon nodded. "I think it is going to be different for us somehow. I may be wrong, but I think times really are changing. They were all a bit like the Musketeers, all for one and one for all. But the way things are moving now ... well, it's more than just not following your father into the docks."

"That where your family work?"

"Yep, loads of them," Jon laughed. "Although I don't hear much talk about work. Nicking tea and covering for each other so they get days off, but actual work … don't seem like there's too much of that gets done! Still, good luck to them. But I think for us there are going to be times when you really just have to look after number one. Get a better job, better house, better life. Yet at the same time, I don't want to get all silly-selfish and leave all that do-right-by-others stuff behind, you understand?"

"Yeah. Yeah I do," Keith nodded. "And surely, this old greek guy, he has to accept that people get it wrong sometimes?"

"Yeah, that's fair. He says you got to aim for a balance and that has to include a balance between wanting to do good and knowing you can't be perfect."

"I think intentions matter," Keith offered. "I mean, say I get sloshed and start acting the arse over something or other, saying all sorts of stupid things. Doesn't it still count for me that I did good things when I wasn't pissed?"

"Course it does. Well, I say it does," Jon assured. "I mean, it's obvious that a good man can't always do good. It's just as obvious that a bad dude might occasionally do someone a decent turn, but that shouldn't blind us to what he's normally like. So, yeah, you got to judge a man in the round. And yeah, as I see it, intentions are key. It's what we're trying to do with our lives that marks us out. What sort of a man we're trying to be."

"Well Jimmy?" Keith asked. "You've gone all silent."

"Yeah …" Jimmy replied thoughtfully while pulling the roach from his dead reefer. "You keep these?" he asked of Jon.

"No way. How do I know where your mouth's been!"

"Fair enough," Jimmy smiled, stamping the remnants into the dirt. "You were right, well nice weed. Seriously!"

"So come on kid, what you make of this Aristotle cat?" Keith prodded.

"Well, mostly like Jon says, his stuff is important. Makes you think. I mean, the thing about intentions, what you really mean to do. Well, I guess it's easy to forget when you're wrapped up in the right now, having a good time, that sort of thing, don't you find?"

"Yeah, I suppose," Keith nodded. "But fair play where it's deserved, you always come across as a guy that thinks things through."

"Do I?" Jimmy asked sceptically. "Well look, here's a thing. Let's say there's this decent dude. Sure, he's been a prat at times but he's growing up, trying his best. He sticks by his mates, looks after people when he can ..."

"We talking about this Mikey again?" Jon asked.

"No. No, not him."

"Alright. So, there's this guy, trying his best. But?" Jon prompted.

"But he's got this girl see. Well, she's not a girl. I mean, she's twenty-seven and ..."

"She's married?"

"Yep. She's married. But she says it's all cool. She's doing what she wants to do and he's not to worry, she's happy. And sure, he's happy too. I mean, a fuck's a fuck, right?" Jimmy laughed without finding anything he'd said amusing.

"Go on," Jon suggested.

"It's a problem, isn't it?" Jimmy suggested. "I mean, for all that one cat's happy enough getting his leg over and the girl's happy with that too, there's the other guy. It really doesn't matter whether the husband is a decent fella or a total arse, does it. In this instance, he's blameless. So the whole thing is wrong, unjust?"

"Hmm," Keith sighed. "Like I said, you think too much!"

"You know this girl?" Jon asked of Keith.

"Yeah, I know her."

"And what he says true? She cool with it all?"

"Honest truth? I'm not all the way sure. I mean, nothing Jimmy's said is off. But I think maybe she's starting to get a bit beyond it's all a bit fun. My guess is, that's what's really going on here. Am I right?" he asked of Jimmy.

"Yes and no," he replied, shaking his head slowly. "I suppose yes, inasmuch as I never thought it'd lead anywhere. The age thing, the married thing … but, well I now see the harm I could be doing. For her and him."

"Course, we don't know he's suffering any harm?" Jon put in.

"I'm shagging his missus!"

"So you said. But unless I missed it, you didn't say he knows that?"

"Well, no," Jimmy considered. "No, I'm as good as certain he doesn't."

"So the harm you're doing him is only potential. I mean, I understand the basic point - if he knew he'd be seriously hacked-off or worse. But right now, you're not actually hurting him. Nor, more to the point, wanting to?"

"Well no, I'm not keen on him finding out!"

"Big guy?" Jon laughed.

"Nah, not as far as I know. But that's not the point."

"I know it's not," Jon nodded. "The obvious assumption is he's going to feel pretty low - to say nothing of let down by her - if it all comes out. But right now, it hasn't. Which brings us to the second potential harm: she starts wanting more, you have it on your toes. Then you feel a right shit."

"And she thinks you're a right shit too!" Keith smiled.

"Exactly," Jimmy nodded. "Whichever way this goes, it ends badly."

"Well, not whichever way," Jon pondered. "I mean," he giggled mischievously, "for all you know, this fling of hers could have put a new spark in the marriage. Before she started shagging you she and her old man might have been like cat and dog all day, cold as fish all night. Now, she's got her mojo super hot he's getting more than he's ever known. Win : win they call that."

"There you go Jimmy boy," Keith smiled. "You're doing the man a favour!"

"Oh yeah, what a guy I am!" Jimmy laughed without meaning it.

"So what does your Aristotle say about all this then?" Keith asked of Jon.

"Well, sad to say … not much!" Jon smiled. "Well, not directly. But his ideas on what is and is not a good and decent thing to do always seek the middle ground. You know, don't go wasting all your money thinking it'll buy you friends, but don't be a tight-wad either. Seems to me, if we want to defend this wife-stealing dude, we have to ask about his intentions, which we've done …"

"Not totally honourable, are they?" Keith posed.

"No, bit selfish in truth. But not completely so, least not according to him."

"Eh?"

"According to your boy here," Jon continued. "The lady's said not to worry. She's cool with things as they are. Sure, there's the worry she might be about to change her mind and look for something more in the future. But she and the dude started this knowing what was what. So in answer to our second question …"

"Which is?"

"What's best for her?"

"OK."

"Seems we might be able to say she's getting that. Really, the effect of all this on her husband is down to her. Sure, he'll blame Jimmy, but deep down he'll know that the real blame is shared somewhere between him and his wife. She's got her reasons for playing away, and he has to be one of them."

"There you go Jimmy, you're in the clear."

"Not quite," Jimmy answered. "Fact is, the more I think about all this the more I'm not that happy with me."

"Ah, now that's the rub," Jon nodded. "In the end, the first judge of whether we're leading a decent life, doing the right things, is us."

"Exactly," Jimmy nodded.

"So come on then," Jon laughed. "What's all this got to do with Penny?"

"Who said ..." Jimmy tried to protest.

"No-one *said*," Keith smiled. "But we all knew there had to be some kind of connection."

"Well actually, I don't think that's fair. I mean, fact is I do worry that I've fucked things up for Sally and that in the end she, her husband and I are all going to feel bad about it. That's not such a great feeling."

"No. OK. I respect that. But beneath it you're clearly saying Sally's not the long-term one. Why not?"

"Because she's ..."

"Can't say married. She can get out of that nowadays," Jon put in. "And you can't say too old - that's not stopping you right now."

"This morning," Jimmy nodded acceptingly, "my mum was on about Penny. Saying what a nice girl she is and ... and well basically saying I should try my luck. Now, like I said, she doesn't like Mikey so that was part of it but ... Well, I suppose the bottom line is I do like her. We get on well and ..."

"And the problem is you think Mikey's a good mate so you can't do it to him, whereas Sally's old man is an unknown so what's the worry?" Keith suggested.

"Well, I suppose that is what I did think."

"Did? What about now?" Jon asked.

"I dunno," Jimmy sighed. "I think part of the reason I am starting to feel bad about the thing with Sally is because, whilst I don't know her husband - as in, I've never met him - on the rare occasions she's said anything about him I've ended up thinking: sounds like an OK guy."

"Whereas Mikey?"

"Is not good enough for Penny, full-stop," Keith proclaimed with untypical certainty.

"That's my mum's view," Jimmy smiled.

"How about your dad?" Jon asked.

"Well that's the thing. He as good as agrees with my mum, but at the same time it's obvious that he would think me a right shit to try and step between a mate and his girl."

"Well, I can see his point."

"Exactly!" Jimmy put in a little sadly.

"What happened to all that best flute greek stuff?" Keith asked.

"Kind of works better when talking about flutes!" Jon smiled. "Although you're right on one count: what does Penny want? You want I ask her?" he asked of Jimmy with total seriousness.

"What, like: Jimmy said, you fancy ditching that bozo …?"

"Well, I wasn't planning on being quite that tactful!" Jon laughed. "Seriously, I could just talk to her general like, nothing specific. See if any hints come out. Make a judgement for you. Might be wrong, but what have you got to lose?"

"She'll probably think you're making a play," Keith suggested.

"Listen, I've only just met her so I'm not wanting to cause any trouble …"

"But?"

"Your man Mikey means nothing to me," Jon grinned. "And not only is she very nice to look at, from the little time I spent with her I'd say she's an interesting girl. Be good to be around."

"Yeah, she is actually," Jimmy nodded.

"See!" Jon smiled.

"Oh don't get me wrong, I think she's great. She works near me. We sometimes meet for a coffee and it's like … well, you spend half an hour with her and you don't want it to end. I took her home one time. We'd both had parties at work so I said we'd meet - didn't want her catching a late bus on her own. It felt good. We had to change at London Bridge and I felt these eyes on me, jealous like, thinking she and I …"

"Guess the problem's the same for her in reverse though," Keith suggested.

"She only know you guys through him?" Jon asked.

"Yep," Keith nodded. "She knew Dawn, but we didn't know her. That right Jimmy?"

"Uh-huh."

"All the more reason I should talk to her."

"Nah, really, I'm not sure," Jimmy sighed. "Bottom line is, I wouldn't feel good even if it was totally what she wanted. Not with him moping around."

"Haven't you got to look after yourself some time?" Keith pondered.

"But that is what I'm doing. Like Jon said, if we think we're leading a shit's life chances are everyone else agrees."

"But what if everyone actually thinks he's the shit. What if everyone agrees with your mum. Penny's too good for him. What if she says it herself, dumps the prat?"

"He's still my mate."

"So what would make him not your mate?" Jon asked.

"I … I don't know, I mean …"

"No, I understand you haven't been thinking it. But think it now. Again, I've only just met the geezer so what do I know. But it's as clear as the wart on my Aunt Greta's nose that he's a bullshitter."

"That wart take its time growing?" Keith asked.

"Now you mention it, yeah."

"Same with Mikey. As kids the three of them, him, Jimmy and Pete were all OK. Used to come down the garage sometimes and lark about, but they were alright," Keith continued. "But Mikey … he's not the guy he was, Jimmy," he said, looking hard into his friend's eyes now. "People change, some for the better, some not. All that blood brothers stuff meant something when it meant something. But you know yourself you'd still trust Pete for anything, with anything. How about Mikey?"

"I know what you're saying."

"Tell me this," Jon put in. "We think this - Sally's her name, right?" he asked of Keith.

"Uh-huh."

"We think this Sally's old man is probably OK, but let's say he's found out. Found out today. When we get back we learn he's knocked her about over it. What d'you do?"

"Easy. I go round and case him."

"And if Mikey did anything to Penny?"

"Yeah, OK, the same."

"So what this all comes down to is this: you think it wrong to do a friend an ill-turn unless he does something bad to you or someone you care about?"

"Well, yes, of course."

"Well, I still think you're missing a big, big point. She might be looking this very moment for a way out and you're not offering it. That's failing her. She looked pissed off with him to me."

"Me too," Keith echoed.

"Exactly. Sooner or later you have to ask what she really wants. What's best for her. Still, meanwhile, we have at least cleared up one thing," Jon smiled.

"Oh yeah, and what's that?" Jimmy asked.

"She's sure got a hold on you!"

Chapter 6

Got my mojo working,
But it just won't work on you
Got my mojo working
But it just won't work on you
I wanna love you so bad
Till I don't know what to do.

Got My Mojo Working
Muddy Walters

Toby had a grin to shame any feline from Cheshire. He also would not stop talking, which worried Jimmy and Pete to the point that they both told him, if he didn't shut the fuck up they were going to throw him in the first biker haunt they came to and leave him to it. Better that than have Penny find out where he'd really been.

The Barn Blues Club was tucked away down an alley at the top of West Street and reached by an open and somewhat rickety iron staircase. The main hall was a good size, with the house band at one end, a make-shift bar at the other, space to dance near the front, tables and chairs scattered around the side for those just wanting to chat or take in the music.

There were maybe a hundred and fifty people in there already, maybe a few more. The first Jimmy saw that he recognised were the cousins from Bexley and Hayes. Two of them had pulled an OK pair of girls, meaning the other two were looking decidedly left out.

"Hey guys," one of them called out in an accent that seemed to have got posher now he'd had a couple of beers.

"You cool?" Jon asked.

"Yeah, sure. Been here an hour or so. Decent place," the other replied.

"So we were told," Pete nodded. "Local boy said, anyway. Band been good?"

"Yeah. Played some good stuff. Muddy Waters, Howlin' Wolf, bit of soul. Stuff we'd never heard too. Should be back on shortly."

"Yeah, right," Pete nodded again. "Your mates OK?" he asked, watching one losing his tongue over against the wall.

"Seems like," both of them laughed.

"Yeah, well. Never know, maybe some more local girls will move on in here?" Jimmy suggested optimistically.

"Bound to, as soon as they hear you're in town!" Jon smiled.

"Yeah, we'll see," one of the boys replied with no obvious sign of expectancy.

"OK. Catch you later," Jimmy promised, seeing Manny over the far side of the hall.

"You alright big man?" Toby asked as they all reached Manny, who was standing alone with a bottle of some unpronounceable French beer.

"All the better for seeing you guys," Manny smiled while nodding ruefully to Mikey and Stevie sat down like a pair of wallflowers, looking fed-up.

"Penny and Dawn?" Jimmy asked.

"Touch of nose powdering. They've been dancing happily enough though. Been OK here really."

"What's that you're drinking?" Jon asked.

"Crow-Ning-Something, French. Alright though."

"That all they got?"

"This or Courage Pale Ale!" Manny laughed.

"Guess we'll go French then!" Jon smiled back. "Get you another?"

"Yeah, thanks."

"Guys?" Jon asked.

"Come on, I'll give you a hand," Jimmy offered.

Two rather podgy and slightly tipsy girls with country-sounding accents started chatting Jimmy and Jon while they waited in the short queue.

"I'm Vanessa," said one. "This is Billie."

"Billie?" Jon asked.

"Yeah. Well, name's Wilhelmina. What would you do?" the second girl laughed, rather cutely in fact.

"Hmm …" Jimmy pondered.

"I asked my mum why. She said she thought it was unusual."

"Make her right, don't you?" Vanessa suggested, a little unkindly.

"You know what, I think Billie's a cute name," Jimmy smiled. "Course, it's also my dad's name."

"Yeah, but I bet he's with a y. I'm ie. Classier I reckon," Billie claimed.

"No doubt about that," Jimmy agreed.

"So, you gonna buy us a drink?" Vanessa asked rather brashly.

"We were just about to do that very thing," Jon lied while throwing Jimmy a questioning look.

"So what will it be?" Jimmy asked, replying to Jon with a nod that was intended to say: Billie, maybe; Vanessa, no way.

"Vodka and tonic," Vanessa burst, downing the last of her tumbler.

"And what about you, Billie," Jon asked with super-charm, the glint in his eye throwing down the challenge to Jimmy.

"She's on gin," Vanessa answered, distracting Jon's attention.

"Is that with tonic or bitter lemon?" Jimmy asked the better looking and, by some distance, less disagreeable girl.

"Tonic course …" Vanessa insisted.

"Is it nice with bitter lemon?" Billie asked.

"Yeah, and well classy too," Jimmy smiled, stepping half a pace to put himself between Billie and Jon now. "All the posh girls drink it that way up town."

"Where you two from then?" Vanessa asked.

"Clapham," Jon answered while shuffling to the front of the queue.

"That posh?" she asked of Jimmy.

"Parts of it are, especially where Jon there lives," he smiled, pointing to his friend's back. "He makes films, you've probably heard of him."

"Really?"

"Jon Parker. Gonna be big-time."

"Really," a now star-struck Vanessa nodded, stepping forward to stand next to Jon.

"And what about you?" Billie asked.

"Me? Boring really, I work in a bank."

"In London? My cousin works in a bank up there. Maybe you know her?"

"Sure, bound to," Jimmy nodded with wry smile while passing on the gin and small bottle of bitter lemon Jon was holding out.

"So, you think you'll dance with me when the band gets back?" Billie asked.

Jimmy looked at her carefully and sympathetically. For all that she was a bit chubby with too much make up and a too-tight and too-short dress, there was something gentle and sweet about her blue eyes and dimpled chin. More than that - and unlike Vanessa - she didn't really seem that cheap or tarty. Her friend, yes, she definitely did seem both. The kind of girl who always finds it hard to get a girlfriend to go out with her more than a few times simply because she always ends up embarrassing herself and those she's with.

"Well Billie, I'll tell you the truth. I mangled my shoulder on the way down - came off the scooter ..."

"No! You poor thing. You broke anything?"

"I don't think so ..."

"You want me to check? I'm training to be a nurse."

"Are you now?" Jimmy smiled, remembering stories he'd heard about nurses. "Well, like I said, I don't think I've broken anything. Just a bit sore."

"You been in all that fighting too?"

"Well, that's the other thing I was going to say. All of which is a total shame because I'm alright as a dancer, even if I say so myself."

"Wanna just talk then?" she asked, a little pleadingly.

"That'd be nice," Jimmy smiled. "Tell you what. Jon and me have got to take these drinks back to some friends, and they'll want a bit of chat. But later, I'll come and find you, promise."

"You sure you promise?"

"I've just bought you a gin and bitter lemon!" Jimmy smiled.

"Thought your mate did that!"

"Oh yeah! OK, I'll get the next one."

"You know she'll be hanging around now, waiting, don't you," Jon suggested as they walked back to the guys, each carrying three dark green bottles of expensive, imported beer.

"I know, I was … well, I wasn't really trying or anything. You interested?"

"We'll see. I'm certainly going to give the other one a wide berth though. Looks a right slag."

"Yep! Could have saved Toby a few quid there mind!"

"That is true, but my guess is he's less chance of catching something he couldn't tell his sister about with a professional!"

"You haven't bought him a beer," were the less than friendly words Penny greeted Jimmy and Jon with.

"Seriously, it's little more than fizzy water," Jon tried. "I mean, it's French …"

"Jon, you seem like a decent guy. My advice is: choose better company."

"Penny," Jimmy tried.

"It's OK, I'm not serious," she replied smilingly. "He seems all in one piece so I guess a little fun won't do him any harm."

"Yeah, right," Jimmy nodded a little too quickly. "That's what we thought. I mean, he's been good as gold so, like you say …"

"Jimmy," Penny interrupted. "When you babble, I get suspicious."

"Best I shut the fuck up then!" he grinned nervously.

"Indeed, best you do. Band's back, you wanna dance? Come on Dawnie," she called, turning without waiting for Jimmy's reply.

Jimmy tried his best to look less than embarrassing alongside Dawn and Penny, Jon, Pete, Keith, Toby and Charlie as the band kicked through *Dust My Broom*, *Smokestack Lightning* and *Respectable.* He cut as the band slipped into a bit of a rave-up, walking over to Mikey, Stevie and Manny standing by the table they'd pretty much locked themselves to.

"Worn out kiddo?" Manny shouted over the band.

"Guess so," Jimmy nodded. "Still aching to tell you the truth."

"You sure you're OK?" Mikey asked with genuine concern, even though it was clear also that he was trying to rebuild a bit of respect after the earlier fall-out.

"Well, reckon I'll be better tomorrow," Jimmy suggested as the singer threw himself into *Come On*.

"Good band," Stevie offered, tapping his bottle to the beat.

"Yeah, I think," Jimmy agreed. "Definitely seen worse. What they called?"

"Said The Giants," Manny smiled. "Guess that's a joke!"

"I guess," Jimmy nodded, looking back to watch the singer - who was the shortest of a short bunch - carry off a cool harmonica solo. "Still, we're all lilliputians next to you!"

"Eh?"

"Never mind ..."

"Thought you said you couldn't dance."

"What, sorry?" Jimmy replied, turning to face a rather sad looking Billie. "I ... well, I wasn't exactly much use."

"She your girl then?" Billie asked, nodding across to Penny.

"No. No, she's my mate here's girlfriend."

"Oh right. So why's he not dancing with her?"

"Because even with a mangled leg and shoulder I'm better than him!" Jimmy laughed.

"Yeah, OK then," Billie replied sceptically. "You still wanna talk?"

"Yeah, sure, in a moment, yeah? Where's your friend, Vanessa?"

"Not sure. Went off with some bloke."

"She like that?" Jimmy asked, without waiting for the easily anticipated answer. "Why you with her?"

"She asked me. Said it'd be OK."

"Yeah, well, it is, don't you think? Nice place this, I'd say."

"Yeah, I guess. I was … I was just going for a wee," the girl explained with a curious hint of something else in her eye.

Jimmy looked at her quizzically while quickly scanning the hall, spotting Vanessa wrapped around some old-looking guy with his hand halfway up her skirt.

"Look, Billie, you …" he began, trying to think of the best way to tell the girl she didn't need to be like her friend.

He could have been wrong, but there seemed to be something too trusting - or too dim - about her. Jane had understood him on reputation and all that easily, but that was because she was a bright girl. Billie, in comparison, seemed dangerously naive.

"Tell you what," he suggested brightly. "You go and do what you gotta do and in a moment I'll get us another drink. OK?"

"OK," the girl sighed, turning without another word and heading off towards an open corridor just past the bar.

"Pulled again kid?" Mikey asked.

"Yeah, well," Jimmy replied a little distractedly, a little ruefully. "She seems a nice enough girl, but she's here with this right dog."

"And the problem with that is?" Mikey laughed boorishly.

"The problem is she's obviously lonely. Meaning she'll end up doing something she'll regret."

"Yeah, well …" Mikey sneered while looking out to watch Penny dancing some kind of twist with Jon and Charlie. "I tell you one thing," he continued, "those friends of yours had better be OK."

"Or what?" Jimmy laughed.

"Yeah, or what!"

"Sure, whatever," Jimmy smiled dismissively before turning to Manny. "Wanna give me a hand getting some more drinks?"

"Sure kid, no problem."

"So," Manny said after a moment or two's silence while they waited in the short queue. "Why's Toby looking like Christmas has come early?"

"Is he? I hadn't noticed," Jimmy tried to lie. "Just happy, I guess."

"Yeah, sure, must just be that," the big guy smiled. "Can't have anything to do with what I heard Pete and that Charlie talking then?"

"I've no idea, Manny. What did you hear them talking about?"

"Well, if I had to guess, I'd say Cilla's!"

"No! You sure? Shit, you turn your back …" Jimmy sighed despairingly. "Right, our turn, what the girls drinking?"

Having helped Manny deliver G&Ts for Penny and Dawn and more Kronenbourgs for the boys, Jimmy walked back to where he assumed he'd find Billie.

Sat on her own with an empty glass she looked even more forlorn. And not just that, she looked both uncomfortable and out of place. Besides being a bad fit, her dress just didn't suit her. She had a boyishness about her, in the roundness of her face, the waviness of her hair, the squareness of her shoulders. She also had a rather unladylike way of sitting, which explained why two guys standing by the bar were staring.

"There," Jimmy said, offering her a fresh tumbler of gin with ice.

"Oh, right, thanks," she sang with surprise, watching as Jimmy eased himself into the chair next to her.

"Still no sign of Vanessa?"

"She's ... er ..."

"What?" Jimmy asked, looking around.

"Think she went down there with some guy," Billie smiled thinly, nodding towards the toilets.

"Oh, right. Yeah, well, they seemed to be getting close earlier."

"Not him," Billie corrected, taking the small bottle of bitter lemon from Jimmy's hand and emptying it into her glass.

"Oh, right," Jimmy nodded a little glumly. "Look, Billie, I'm sure you know this anyway but ..."

"You're going to say she's easy, aren't you?"

"Well," Jimmy laughed, looking into the girl's rather sweet eyes. "Yes!"

"I know. But then again, she gets plenty of attention. Always gets taken out."

"Billie, she's a slag. That's why she gets lots of attention. Bet she doesn't often get asked out by the same guy twice though."

"I wouldn't know."

"No? Well take it from me, she doesn't. And why we're on this, put your knees together."

"Sorry?"

"There are two guys over there and they've been staring up your dress for the past five minutes. That's enough, don't you think?"

"Why you!" she snapped.

"I'm just trying to be nice here, Billie. You deserve better than that. Than them."

She looked across to the guys by the bar then to her legs, pressing her thighs tight together while trying to push the hem of her dress down. "Stupid thing, I told her I'd look dumb."

"Vanessa?"

"Yeah. It's hers. Said I needed to look the part if I wanted to make out."

"Make out being her way of saying get some cat's hand inside your knickers," Jimmy suggested cruelly before taking a swig from his bottle of Kronenbourg.

"Yeah, well, she was wrong, wasn't she," Billie replied sadly, her eyes looking dull now. "I mean, that's not happening."

"That what you want? That the kind of girl you want to be? Go over and see them. I'm sure they'll be happy to take turns."

"Don't be horrible," she sighed.

"I'm trying to be nice," Jimmy repeated.

"Yeah, well, thanks. You better get back to your girlfriend."

"Billie, like I said, she isn't my girlfriend. But you're right, I do have one."

"Yeah, I guessed. Could have just …"

"What? Had a little fun? A kiss and grope. You reckon you'd feel good about that in the morning?"

She looked at him with a blank, expressionless face for a moment before whispering a barely audible "No. Sorry. Guess I've had too much to drink. You are nice, Jimmy. Thanks."

"That's OK. So, what you going to do now," he started to ask before noticing the two cats from Hayes or Bexley or wherever the hell they were from joining the bar line.

"Look, you want to meet a couple of decent guys, just to chat. Maybe dance a little?"

"Two? How's that going to work?"

"I'm not saying anything will work. They're at a loose end. You too. So just be friends. They won't jump you or anything, promise."

"Well …" she began.

"Guys," Jimmy called across, the room relatively quiet now the band were on another break.

"You cool?" the taller, fairer one asked.

"Sure, course, all's well. Listen, this is Billie and she's … well, she needs someone to dance with. And I say, why say one when you can have two?"

"Hello Billie," the second guy smiled a little shyly. "Paul."

"George," the other one offered.

"See, what I tell you?" Jimmy smiled to Billie. "Too posh too be anything but decent."

"OK, but where are you …"

"I'm just going to join my friends for a bit. Catch up with you later?"

"Yeah, OK," Billie replied, a little sadly, a little uncertainly.

"Just be nice to her, she's a bit low," Jimmy whispered in George's ear. "Don't take advantage, you hear?"

"Sure, of course, who you think we are?" the guy replied, a tad hurt.

"Yeah, sorry. It's just … well, I don't know how it's happened, but she's here with this right slapper and she might just be silly enough to be like her. She needs her own knights-errant to save her from herself! Be good to her."

"Sure, promise."

As Jimmy started back towards his table he all-but bumped into Mikey and Stevie headed the other way.

"Just popping out for a smoke, wanna join us?" Mikey asked.

"Nah, we did some good weed earlier," Jimmy smiled. "Not that it's done my shoulder much good!"

"You want a heart? Stevie, give the guy a heart."

Stevie pulled a rather prissy little purse thing from his pocket, flipped the catch to offer Jimmy a pick.

"No, honest, you know what, I'm just going to chill with a beer. Maybe try another dance when the band get back on. But thanks."

"You going to put me in one of your films then?" a now quite obviously drunk Vanessa burst, suddenly appearing at Jimmy's back.

"You know what, that's exactly what I was just discussing with my bosses here," Jimmy claimed dead-pan.

"Your bosses?" Vanessa asked, the disbelief in her voice amplified by her wide-eyed and unblinking watching of Billie sitting happily chatting between Paul and George. "Who they?"

"Couple of rich cats from up town. Taken a big shine to your friend," Jimmy smiled mischievously. "The fair guy's dad's this hot-shot business dude. Reckon she'll do OK there!"

"Bitch."

"Yeah, but like I said, these guys …" Jimmy giggled, nodding to Mikey and Stevie.

"Who is she?" Stevie and Mikey asked in unison, looking disapprovingly at Vanessa the way a Duchess might view a chimney sweep.

"I don't know!" Jimmy smiled, turning his back and walking as fast as his dodgy knee would allow.

"Oh, back now are we?" Penny teased, a glow of exertion making her pretty face shine despite the dull lighting.

"I'm on a mission to rescue you from yourself. His Leaderness - also known as soppy-arse I believe - thinks you're going to fly away with Jon and Charlie."

"Does he now? Well, I've heard sillier ideas," she smiled. "So, how you feeling now?"

"Well, tell you the truth, I do feel a bit better. Guess I'm on the mend, might even be up for another dance if I can find someone worth dancing with!"

"Oh, thought that's what you've been sorting," she suggested with a lopsided grin that brought a fetching dimple to her right cheek.

"No. Actually, I've been saving her from herself."

"You know, Jimmy Carlton, anybody else say that and I'd think tosh. But you … you probably mean it."

"I do."

"Yeah, I know you do. Jon said she's alone here with this slut of a mate?"

"She was. I've put her with a couple of guys we met earlier. They're far too suburban to take advantage."

"Are they now?" she mused, the lopsided grin now the other way up. "What about inner-city boys then, they not to be trusted?"

"Never! Lock up your daughters every time."

"I'll have to bear that in mind," she nodded, taking a sip of her tumbler full of now slightly warmed G&T, no ice in sight. "So where is soppy-arse anyway?"

"He and Stevie just went out for a smoke."

"Did they. So, you're my chaperone. Going to save me from your not-to-be-trusted mates …"

"Well ... maybe. Trouble is, they're all mates. I mean, how's a man supposed to choose between them?"

"How indeed!" Penny smiled. "They're alright, aren't they," she added seriously.

"Jon and Charlie you mean?"

"Who else, soppy and his echo?"

"Hmm, I think that's a bit harsh. I heard there was this one time Stevie didn't totally agree with Mikey."

"Really? Oh, I hadn't heard that. Guess I got it all wrong," she nodded thoughtfully.

"But yeah, they are. Me and Pete have met up with them a few times, usually to go down to the Crawdaddy."

"Oh right, I've heard of that. Couple of the guys at work were saying ... they called the Yardbirds or something?"

"Yeah, that's who has been there recently. Not actually seen them. We saw the Stones and then the Kinks, but I'd like to see this new band ..."

"Everyone says their guitar guy is good."

"They do. How'd you know all this?"

"Like I said, couple of guys at work are into their music. You listen, you learn, that's how the world works Jimmy," she smiled. "Not just a pretty face, see!"

"No," Jimmy smiled broadly, impressed and just a little smitten. "Sorry, who said you had a pretty face?"

"Let me think now," she replied, a finger pressed to the corner of her mouth, her big, hazel eyes scanning the ceiling. "Oh yeah ... You!"

"Me? Shit. Chaperone's supposed to say something like that?"

"Good question. I reckon something like that could lose you your job."

"No way! You're not gonna tell on me, are you?"

"Well, that depends," Penny smiled, her eyes now watching as the band reassembled on stage.

"On what?"

"On what these guys play next …"

"Eh?" Jimmy asked dumbly before the first bars of *Got My Mojo Working* burst out.

"Yeah, this'll do. Come on," she insisted, pulling him through the crowd.

It was the strangest, most intense and unsettling, exhilarating and intoxicating dance Jimmy had ever known. No, it was the strangest, most intense and unsettling, exhilarating and intoxicating *moment* he'd ever known. Ever in his life. Full stop.

Within seconds, he felt kind of entranced by Penny. By the brightness of her eyes. By the almost supernatural luminosity of those golden halos around her deep, dark, well-pool pupils. More than that, her lips seemed to glow a fiery red as she sang along to Muddy Waters' words, pointing accusingly at Jimmy while shaking her head in perfect time with the beat: *but it just don't work on you*.

And then she started making a kind of mask of her fingers. Two horizontal Vs which she dragged one after the other across her face, hiding and then revealing those special, staring, shimmering eyes. Tempting and teasing him.

He copied her every move, every flick of the hips, turn of the feet, quiver of the leg, shrug of the shoulders, shake of the head, pout of the lips, wiggle of the nose, gaze of the eyes. He copied her teasing over the chorus, accusing her of being the impervious one, the rejectionist, the cold heart to his warm mojo-rising.

As he mirrored her he felt her. Not by touch but in the movement of the air around him. Air that her grace and seductiveness was caressing and inspiring, moving and arousing. The air between them seemed like theirs to play with. To push against the other. To use to tell the other that those words might just lie.

"Got my mojo working but it just don't work on you," he burst out loudly, leaning towards her, his shoulders shuffling while his head stayed perfectly still, his eyes gazing hard and unblinking into hers.

And she mirrored him, leaning forward also, her hips moving against the rhythm of her shoulders, pushing her slim waist out one side, then the other, all the while keeping her head steady, her eyes fixed.

They were oblivious to those around them. To Dawn, Toby and Pete to their side; to Billie, Paul and George behind them. They were oblivious to the looks they were attracting. Looks of admiration, jealousy and not a little inadequacy.

For everyone around them, the sheer obsessive exclusiveness of their interest in each other felt overwhelming. The sensual symmetry of their intense connection an exemplar to which on-one else could possibly aspire.

Then the band slipped into *So Many Roads*, slowing everything down, adding a new feel with a moody harmonica behind the tingling guitar.

They moved like wild cats stalking prey in slow motion, like cobras coiling around something delectable. Without touching they touched each other more deeply than either had ever connected with another soul.

"So many roads, so many trains to ride," Penny sang, her actions miming a slow train with such a sultry sexiness it sent a chill down Jimmy's spine.

"So many roads, so many trains to ride," he echoed.

"I gotta find my baby," she smiled, her white teeth catching the light, her whole face radiating warmth and uplifting beauty.

"Before I can be … satisfied," Jimmy nodded, as if to say: Yeah! That's the truth. That's all there is.

"Jimmy!" Paul shouted into Jimmy's ear, while resting a hand on his shoulder.

"Wh-what? What?" Jimmy snapped.

"Billy thinks there's some trouble coming."

"Billie?" Jimmy asked blankly, nodding to the girl still dancing with George.

"No, sorry, my cousin," Paul said, pointing to the rather startled looking guy standing just behind. "This Billy. Something's happening outside."

"What? What's happening?" Jimmy asked, losing all rhythm and concentration.

"Some trouble …"

"What trouble?" an obviously annoyed and disorientated Penny asked.

"Problem?" Pete asked.

"Seems like. Look, let's just step away a second," Jimmy suggested irritably.

"Seems some East End kid's got killed or something," Billy explained as they walked away from the dancers. "There's a crowd of them outside. Don't know why but they think someone in here's got something to do with it."

"But that's …" Jimmy gasped, shaking his head in incomprehension while holding Penny close without realising it. "Well, we don't want any part of whatever it is. This is a decent place, they don't need …"

"Jimmy, let's go, yeah?" Penny said. "We'll find somewhere else."

"Yeah, sure, you're right …"

"Trouble?" Manny asked, joining them.

"Seems there could be. Look, would you just go with Billy and Paul here. See what's to see."

"I'm sorry kiddo," Jimmy said while watching the guys heading towards the main entrance.

"Not your fault."

"No, maybe not this time, but like you said earlier, this is all a lot of Boy's Own crap. Oh well, let's get everyone together," Jimmy sighed, noticing for the first time that his best friend's girlfriend was resting her chin on his shoulder, her warm slim body curved perfectly into his.

By the time they'd all got together by their table there was a worried buzz creeping around the hall. Even the band had picked it up, stopping midway through a second Otis Rush number Jimmy couldn't remember the name of anyway.

"Guys on the door reckon there's maybe thirty of them," Manny explained as he, Paul and Billy got back. "They say this kid that's dead got some bad speed off a dude in here."

"How'd he die?" Keith asked.

"Fell off that fire escape thing," Manny replied glumly. "They're all down there, bottom of the stairs, waiting for an ambulance or something. Guys here have locked the doors and basically seem to be just hoping for the best."

"You reckon the doors will hold if they decide they want to get in?" Jimmy asked.

"Nope."

"We need to get out of here," Penny insisted.

"Not sure how though," Manny mused. "I mean, looks like one way in, one way out."

"No," Billie put in a little timidly. "There is another way. You can get across the roof into the Zodiac ..."

"What's that?" Dawn asked.

"It's a coffee bar, biggish place."

"Any chance these guys will make for that next?"

"Well, I suppose …" Billie replied apologetically. "I was just saying …"

"Billie, thanks," Jimmy smiled. "We're lucky to have you. How d'you know that anyway?"

"Used to come here Saturday mornings for a dance club," the girl replied proudly.

"Right, well unless anyone has a better idea?" Jimmy asked, quickly scanning the sea of faces. "Nope, right, let's follow Billie to this coffee place."

"Where's Mikey?" Toby asked.

"He not …" Manny began, quickly checking the group.

"Stevie," Jimmy called to the guy hanging sheepishly behind Jon, Charlie and Keith. "You know?"

"Er, he, er … I think he was talking to someone down by the khazi."

"Come on, show me," Jimmy barked. "Manny, you want to help get everyone out?"

"What about you?" Penny asked.

"Which way is it Billie?"

"See that door just by the side of the stage. Through that's this long corridor. Go right to the end and there's some stairs. Up gets you to the roof. There's only one way."

"OK. I'll find it."

"I'll come with you," Pete volunteered.

"So," Jimmy asked of Stevie as they walked down the poorly lit and none-too-pleasant smelling passage towards the toilets. "Who, exactly, was he talking to?"

"That girl."

"Not that Vanessa?"

"Uh-huh."

"Who's Vanessa?" Pete asked, half guessing the answer.

"Some slag," Jimmy sneered. "Right, Pete, stay here. You see him, shout," he suggested before turning to Stevie. "You, you come with me."

It didn't take them long. There were only four guys at the urinals and all bar one of the traps were open. And the gruff voice that replied to the bang on the one closed door was definitely not Mikey.

"No joy?" Pete asked as they returned.

"Nope. What you reckon?"

"Try the Girls'?"

"Could do," Jimmy pondered uncertainly while turning again to Stevie. "Anywhere else he might've gone?"

"Not ... not that I can think," the guy replied timidly.

"Right, this time, you stay here. You see him, you shout. Don't do that and I'll break your arms. Come on Pete."

Gingerly, the two of them popped their heads around the door. First thing they noticed was just how different - and cleaner - the place was.

"What the ..." a tall girl with reddish hair snapped on seeing them.

"Look, sorry," Jimmy smiled, holding his hands out wide, palms up as if to show he was both apologetic and unthreatening. "We're looking for someone."

"Fuck off," she snapped.

"No, serious. Look, you seen a girl in here with a ..."

"Bloke?" she sniggered. "Let me think," she continued, play-acting. "How about, course you dope!"

"Now?"

"Now?" she echoed, quickly looking round. "Don't think so. Look, if you're after finding your girlfriend wait outside."

"We're after the guy. His girlfriend *is* waiting outside," Pete explained.

"Oh," the girl replied ruefully. "Wait there." She came back less than thirty seconds later having disappeared down one side of the space. "Try the last two down the end, something in both I think."

"Thanks," Jimmy smiled sweetly. "We owe you."

"Yeah, sure. I'll send you my bill," the girl laughed, leaving.

Two other girls appeared from cubicles as Jimmy and Pete walked down the line, each accepting a finger over lips request for understanding and silence. Then, as they neared the end an instantly startled guy and girl stepped from the second to last door.

"Not a fucking word," Pete whispered, he and Jimmy now standing in front of the remaining closed door.

"Mikey, you there?" Jimmy asked, nicely enough, watching the startled couple all-but running to the exit.

Silence.

"Mikey, open the door or we kick it in," Pete said more menacingly.

"No, no … it's …" came a mumbled reply.

Without another word Jimmy kicked the door open. Mikey stood with his back to them, his strides half-way down his legs, the tail to his shirt not quite covering his pale, flabby arse.

"You dirty cunt," Pete snarled.

"What the fuck," Vanessa gasped, pulling her mouth from Mikey's penis.

"Get up and get the fuck out of here," Jimmy ordered while dragging Mikey from the cubicle and pushing him face-first against the brick wall.

"And not a word to anyone," Pete added as the girl got up from the closed toilet seat, wiped her lips, straightened her dress and staggered past.

"Go and get Stevie," Jimmy said coldly, calmly.

"OK, you … you sure?"

"Please Pete. Just do it, yeah?"

When Pete returned with Stevie they found Jimmy leaning nonchalantly against the wall, Mikey in a heap, his trousers still around his knees, one hand around his crotch, the other held pleading out in front of his bloodied, already swollen face.

"I've no issues with you," Jimmy told Stevie. "Unless you've any with me?"

"N-no, course not. Course not Jimmy," the guy replied.

"Fine. We see you around, no problems. Happy to talk or walk on by. But we see him again, then we break something, you understand?"

"Y-yes."

"Good. So, you get him out of here and away from us. OK?"

"Yeah, sure, course, no problem …"

Without another word or glance, Jimmy walked over to one of the wash basins and rinsed the blood off his knuckles. Managed also to pick a few bits of grit from his right palm that had been irritating him all day. Then he and Pete walked out, back into the hall.

People still seemed anxious but the band had started into an uncertain version of *Louie Louie* which Jimmy sang along to in his head, optimistically, as they headed for the door Billie had pointed out: *a fine little girl, she waits for me; me catch the ship across the sea …*

Chapter 7

A fine little girl, she waits for me
Me catch the ship across the sea
I sailed the ship all alone
I never think I'll make it home

Louie Louie, oh baby, me gotta go
Louie Louie, oh baby, me love her so.

Louie Louie
The Kingsmen

But, by the time they walked out onto the roof Jimmy felt both nervous and a little nauseous. The night air was fresher and somehow more salty than earlier. He turned round to stare out towards the sea, the beach dappled by moonlight which caught the tips of the gentle waves as they hit the pebbles, the far distance an inky, formless black.

"You want I explain?" Pete asked quietly.

"I … I'm not sure," Jimmy began, distractedly, the sounds from the town below mixing with the dizziness in his head, confusing and comforting him in equal if paradoxical measure. "I mean, what's to say?"

"Can't just say nothing."

"Why not?" Jimmy asked, half serious, half incapable of considered thought.

The coolness of the night seemed to be easing his pains while making him more lightheaded. His shoulder no longer seemed to ache so much, nor his knee, nor his arm. Only his palm - oddly - seemed to hurt, from where he'd just scratched out those bits of gravel that had been embedded there since the crash. That and his knuckles, although he wasn't really sure whether that was physical pain or a painful memory.

He hadn't hit Mikey that much. Not that many times. Not that hard. Only as much as was necessary to explain: that was it, fuck off, don't want to see you ever again, and you stay away from her too.

But what now? First off, what possible good would it do Penny to know the truth?

Sure, she was a grown woman, capable of looking after her own emotions. Tell her and let her decide what to do with the knowledge. Free will and all that. But what if she were to say: I'm going back to talk to him? How'd that fit with Jimmy's commanding assertion a moment back that he was unwanted, unclean and undeserving; the tainted son of a worthless spiv?

That was the essence of what he'd said - to Mikey and Stevie - but who did he say it for?

Just himself.

So it would just be vanity on his part to try and stop her going back.

But what if the truth really, really upset her? Crippled her confidence. Made her feel worthless with the shame of the abandoned? Didn't Jimmy owe it to her to keep her safe, to protect her from needless harm? Wasn't that part of doing the right thing by the right people?

Or was that just the self-serving tosh of a man who, bottom line, had wanted an excuse to step between the two of them. An excuse to end any debt of friendship to Mikey so he could walk off into an ever-idyllic sunset with the prettiest girl in town.

"Look, I'll, er …" Pete mused. "I'll see …" he offered, walking away slowly towards the small crowd of Dawn, Penny, Toby, Billie, Paul and George waiting some fifty yards ahead across the flat, concrete roof.

Just to their side stood Paul and George's cousins, Billy and … Harry, Jimmy thought the fourth one was called. They were in a quiet huddle with the two girls they'd been with all night.

Nearer, standing against the parapet, Manny, Keith, Jon and Charlie were all looking down into the alleyway.

"Well?' Jimmy asked, joining them.

"The boy's gone," Manny explained, turning to face him. "Seems no doubt he's dead. Ambulance blokes covered him with a blanket then carried the body away."

"Couple of guys went with him," Jon continued. "In the ambulance, I mean."

"A few more have pitched up," Manny added, looking down over the parapet once more. "Looks like maybe fifty down there now. Could all blow over in an hour or so, but I reckon we did right to get away. Billie says we get to this café over there," he finished, waving vaguely towards the corner where West Street met Western Road.

"So where's Mikey?" Keith asked.

"Not here."

"You mean you didn't find him?"

"No, not that."

"Oh, right," Keith nodded, not really knowing what more to think or say.

"You want to talk about it?" Manny asked quietly, dropping back with Jimmy as they all walked slowly towards the others.

"Not really."

"So you did find him?"

"Yep."

"And he's not come, Stevie neither," Manny said for no reason than to hear himself confirm the only known facts.

"They'll make their own way back," Jimmy added.

"Right. Stevie understands then?"

"Uh-huh."

"Look kid, whatever happened I don't doubt you only did what had to be done."

"Why? Why you so sure?"

"Because I know you …"

"Do you? Sometimes I'm not sure I really know myself."

"Jimmy, what is all this?" Manny asked sharply, stopping and holding on to Jimmy's arm to stop him also. "Look, I don't know what happened back there. But then again, I don't need to, do I? He did something that you couldn't accept. It ends there."

"Does it? Why does it? Who am I to say what ends where?"

"Say? You don't *say* as in telling *me* what to think, you clown," Manny snapped. "I say. You decided Mikey's done something you can't forgive. I can't forgive it either. Not because I know what it was. Because I know you."

"But that's my point Manny, that's my fucking point. What if … what if my reasons for doing whatever aren't good ones. Aren't worthy ones?"

"Why wouldn't they be?" Manny asked more slowly, more thoughtfully. His big, brown eyes staring quizzically down into Jimmy's.

"Oh, I don't know. I mean, sometimes … sometimes things get complicated."

"Listen," Manny replied. "You've had a bang on the nut, trashed your scooter and now fallen out with someone you used to call your best friend. Guess you've had better days!" he smiled. "But those are all done things now. Can't be undone. So where's that leave us? Well, for me, nothing's changed. I think you're an alright guy. I like having you as a friend. I trust you. You decided Mikey was in the wrong, end of story as far as I'm concerned."

"That's it?" Jimmy asked. "No questions?"

"Don't get me wrong kid. Nothing's forever. You once thought you and Mikey were blood brothers till the end. Now you're seriously pissed with him. Could happen between us. But right now, here, today … my guess is, whatever it was, it was something I would have found unacceptable too."

"What about Penny?"

"What about her? It was between you and him. She'll have to make up her own mind."

"I … I don't think I can tell her."

"Why … oh," Manny nodded. "Is that what this is all about? You seriously thinking - but for the fact you think she's great and a fuck sight too good for him - you thinking but for that you would have just said: OK Mikey, when you're ready?"

"Well, I mean …" Jimmy tried thoughtfully. "If it'd been someone, you know, without a girl waiting …"

"Exactly! Fucking exactly," Manny insisted, his voice raised enough to attract the attention of those waiting by the now open door down into the Zodiac. "Fucking exactly. Context, Jimmy, that is what this is all about. Some things are fine to do in some circumstances, very much not OK to do in others. If you're telling me that shit was doing something behind her back then I tell you, I see him I'll break whatever you didn't!"

"So you're not worried I maybe lost it because …"

"Because you go silly whenever she's around?" Manny laughed. "I have no doubt whatsoever that if what you're telling me is you hit him, then yeah. I bet you found it easier to do than you otherwise might. But this isn't about the quality of the punch Jimmy. This is about the quality of the man. Dude make a girl like Penny look dumb, take her for granted, he don't deserve second thoughts."

"Actually, I'm not bothered about him. I mean, I never expected to say that, let alone think it. But … well, I guess today was a day for seeing things differently."

"Or just seeing things, Jimmy. Or just seeing things as they are."

"Maybe," Jimmy nodded. "But … no, actually, you're right Manny, thanks. There are no buts. Thing is, just a moment ago I was thinking: what if she thinks I was wrong? What if I tell her and she says: mind you're own business Jimmy. And then goes off to find him?"

"Say she does …"

"I know," Jimmy nodded. "That's what you've just helped me realise. Thanks. She's got her choice to make. I made mine. And there's no undoing it. Sure, I was maybe more angry because of the way I feel about her. But basically, I don't want a slag hunter for a friend. That's it."

"Nor do I," Manny nodded, hugging Jimmy painfully hard, his big left fist crushing the soothing numbness out of his doubly-sore shoulder. "So, you gonna tell her?" he asked, leading them on.

"Nope!"

"Coward!"

"Yep!" Jimmy agreed, adding: "Maybe you …?"

"No way! I'll talk to Dawnie, she'll know what to do," the big guy hoped.

The Zodiac coffee bar ran above a number of the shops opposite the Clock Tower. It was wide - or long, depending on where you start - but not very deep. It was also busy, yet somehow calm. There was a nice vibe. Nothing like the tension they'd left behind in The Barn.

More than that, they got lucky. The stairs down from the roof entered the place in the middle of the long wall opposite the windows. Probably seen as the less cool side, there was already one free table which they started to crowd around only to see another opening up as a foursome got to their feet a little way further down.

"Hi Billie," one of those leaving smiled.

"Hi Alison. You just going?"

"Yeah. I'm on earlies tomorrow. You?"

"No. Off tomorrow. Back in Tuesday."

"OK. Lucky you," Alison smiled jealously before turning and following her friends out.

"Another nurse?" George asked as they gathered around the now free table.

"Yep."

"Think we should move down," he grinned to his brother.

"You should, you'd like it," Billie nodded. "It's OK here."

"I'm sure it is. Then again, you get used to what you've got, don't you. Bexley's a backwater but fact is, I've lived there all my life," Paul shrugged.

"We've got a decent club though," George added. "Get a few top bands ... he's been," he added, nodding down the wall towards the large Wurlitzer Lyric just starting to play Georgie Fame's *Yeah, Yeah*.

"Oh good, I like this," Billie smiled, jigging from side-to-side vaguely in time to the song.

"You been to the Black Prince, Jimmy?" Harry asked.

"Don't think so."

"Sundays it calls itself the Bexley Jazz Club, but basically it's just a big hall out back of the pub."

"Down the A2, right?" Charlie asked.

"That's the place," Harry smiled optimistically.

"Nah. Too far," Charlie grinned dismissively.

"Whereas coming down here?" George asked lightly.

"Is a day out. Not the same thing at all!"

"Got Graham Bond down in a couple of weeks. Paul's band's playing support."

"You in a band, Paul?" Jon asked.

"Yeah, well," the guy replied shyly.

"Wow! Cool," Billie cooed, impressed.

"We're not that great …"

"So why they putting you on?" Jon pressed.

"They're OK," George insisted on his brother's behalf.

"They're better than just OK," Billy and Harry chorused in their cousin's support.

"Won some local talent thing, that's right isn't it?" Billy added.

"Well, yeah," Paul nodded. "But we're just a college band really. We're getting better though."

"What you play?" Jimmy asked.

"Bit like the band we just heard. Bit of R&B, blues. Maybe a bit more soul than them."

"Sounds good, what you called?"

"Ah, yeah, well …"

"Go on," Jimmy pressed.

"Well, not my choice and we've talked of changing it …"

"Go on!" Jimmy laughed.

"The Epitaphs Soul Band."

"What kind of a fucking name is that!" Charlie burst.

"We were trying for something that would sound, you know, kind of weird but interesting …"

"Well, you got it half right!" Charlie laughed.

"Yeah, well," Paul smiled shyly. "We thought it would make people ask: oh yeah, what's that all about then? Like everyone does with The Ram Jam Band …"

"Named after a pub on the A1," Jon explained.

"Sorry, what is?" Jimmy asked.

"The Ram Jam Band. Named after the Ram Jam Inn."

"How you know that?"

"Met them a couple of weeks back. Nice guys. Got this black GI or airman or something singing with them. Great voice."

"Gino Washington," Harry put in. "Paul's almost as good. Honest! Even if he is my cousin."

"So you're the singer," Jimmy nodded. "Get all the girls, they say, singers."

"Is that a fact?" Paul replied doubtfully.

"Actually," Billie mused. "I heard it was more like: they get all the girls a coffee!"

"Oh, yeah, right …"

"Nah, it's OK. My call," Charlie offered.

"No. Actually, I'll go," Billie decided.

"No, honest, it's OK …" George and Paul jousted to say.

"Serious!" she insisted. "You've all been great for me tonight, so I'm going. Besides, this is our town!" she added proprietorially. "Elkie and Carla will give me a hand, won't you girls … you lot can sort out some chairs," she suggested to no-one in particular.

"In that case, I'll go and feed the jukebox," Charlie decided.

"Oh right. Put on F4 for me," Billie smiled pleadingly.

"OK. What is it?"

"The Blues Busters."

"Never heard of them!"

"I tell you," Billie smiled to the girls. "These London boys. So behind the times!"

"So, you think you'll see them again. Maybe come down?" Jimmy asked of Billy and Harry. "What they called, Elkie and Carla?"

"Yeah," Billy nodded, watching the girls walking towards the counter at the far end of the place.

"They're OK," Harry agreed, grabbing a couple of free chairs from behind a neighbouring table.

"And what about you two?" Jon asked of George and Paul. "Going to duel over Billie?"

"Oh yeah, I should think so," George nodded with a grin. "Swords at dawn, I'm thinking."

"Cool," Paul smiled. "I'll go pistols!"

"Sorry George," Jon laughed. "Better look elsewhere for a Second. My money's on Paul!"

"Yeah, well, he's older, what chance have I got! By the way Jimmy, what happened to the other one?" George asked.

"Never mind," Jimmy snapped more sharply than he intended.

"OK ..." the boy began thoughtfully, trying to read Jimmy's look.

"Sorry," Jimmy apologised. "She was just no good. That was why I asked you guys to take care of Billie."

"Yeah, well ..." George nodded, sensing there was more but choosing not to ask. "Oh look! Here's the lady herself," he beamed charmingly as Billie returned with a tray full of coffees and milkshakes, Carla - or was it Elkie - behind with another.

"A lady? Coo-ee, I like that!" Billie giggled, putting her tray down with care.

The three girls squeezed on the narrow bench against the wall, the guys, having managed to snaffle enough chairs, sat in a horseshoe around the table, sharing out the coffees, shakes and bits of shortbread and cake the girls had also thought to get.

"Thank you ladies," Jimmy nodded with exaggerated chivalry. "To Brighton," he added, raising his coffee cup in a toast.

"Jimmy," Billie replied, serious with affection in her eyes. "Thank you. But for you I would have had a right crappy time. Instead, I get to meet all you guys and Carla and Elkie too," she added breezily, her nods distinguishing the pony-tailed Carla from her darker-haired friend.

"You been down here before?" Elkie asked in a surprisingly sultry, husky voice.

"Yeah, a few times," Jimmy replied. "Just for the day like, it's nice. You all from here then?"

"Yep," the three girls chimed in sync.

"Billie says you make films or something," Elkie said to Jon.

"Not quite," he laughed. "That was Jimmy exaggerating. I'd like to, but right now it's just adverts."

"For the telly though?" Carla checked.

"Some. But mostly it's the things they show at the cinema while everyone's off getting an ice-cream or whatever!"

"Still, sounds interesting."

"How about you?"

"Me and Elkie work for the Council here. Rates Department."

"Bet that makes you popular," Charlie smiled.

"Yeah, well, thankfully no-one gets to see us! Still, it's OK really. You know, nice people, pay's alright, what more you want."

"Hmm, well …" Charlie pondered. "Fame, big house, fancy car … course, Paul'll have all that soon, when his band breaks big."

"I wish," the guy grinned.

"You say you're at college?" Jimmy asked.

"Yeah. Art College, Ravensbourne."

"So you can draw as well!" Billie asked, doubly impressed.

"Well, yeah … but not like an artist. I'm doing design. Furniture design right now …"

"No way!" Jimmy burst. "I should put you in touch with my dad and uncle. They're furniture makers. They'd love the chance to work on something other than wardrobes and sideboards!"

"Jimmy's dad's called Billy too," Billie nodded knowingly to Paul's cousin.

"Cool name," the boy smiled.

"And what about you two?" Jimmy asked.

"We're still at school, final year …"

"Final year?" Jimmy repeated quizzically.

"Yeah," Harry nodded.

"They're twins, didn't you see it?" Carla put in.

"Twins … er, no. I mean, brothers, sure but … aren't twins meant to be the same?"

"Not if they're not," Billy answered cryptically.

"Right, well that explains that!" Jon laughed.

"What he means is you can get non-identical twins, like us," Harry explained.

"You at school too George?"

"Yeah, my final year too. We're basically the same age, just a month apart."

"And what're your plans?" Jon asked generally of the three.

"Not sure really," George answered first. "I'm thinking of going to University, maybe … guess first thing is get through my exams. Coming up soon now."

"You?"

"Guess I'm not sure either. Our dad's got this printing company, getting to do a lot of album covers and that sort of thing. Be cool to work on something like that I think … Harry's dead set on becoming a teacher though, aren't you kid?"

"Kid?" Jon smiled.

"Yeah, he's younger by thirty minutes," Billy giggled.

"I reckon that's where my sister'll go, English," Jimmy put in while considering the coincidences of life: furniture making, Sally's old man being a printer, three cousins being as good as the same age.

"I'm thinking History," Harry replied. "How old's your sister?"

"Fifteen."

"Well, time for her to think yet," he offered sage-like.

"Hey! First of mine," Charlie burst as the opening bars of The Kingsmen's *Louie Louie* crackled from the jukebox.

They all tapped and swayed to the simple beat, more or less agreeing on a chorus of: "Louie Lou-i, oh baby, me gotta go, oh-no-no-no. Louie Lou-i, oh baby, me love her so." With some faltering variations, followed by: "a fine little girl she waits for me; me catch the ship across the sea …"

"Any idea of what he's saying?" Jon asked after mumbling something unintelligible for the next couple of lines.

"No idea," Paul shook his head. "And we've rehearsed it!"

"Guess that's the thing though," Jon pondered. "Seeing as no-one's got a clue what they're on about you can sing what you want. Who's to say you're wrong!"

"When's your thing again?" Charlie asked.

"Fortnight."

"You gonna come down then?" Harry asked, optimistically.

"Yeah, I think we might. What you reckon?" Charlie asked of Jon and Jimmy.

"Why not," Jimmy smiled, turning to the still swaying and mumbling trio of Carla, Billie and Elkie. "You all gonna come up?"

"Yeah, let's," Billie smiled, nudging the other two. "Maybe I'll get my cousin to come too," she added before bursting excitedly: "Oh good, here's my song."

"Oh, of course, I know this," Charlie accepted.

The ten new and firm friends sang their happy way through *Soon You'll Be Gone*:

"Soon you'll be gone and I'll be all alone …"

Then they all smiled at each other with happy satisfaction as the song faded away, replaced for a moment by just the hum of voices from around the place as the jukebox fell silent.

Looking across a little, Jimmy saw Penny looking back, her face blank, Dawn saying something in her ear. She knows, he thought. What now?

"Well," Carla began reluctantly. "I think we probably need to get on home."

"You want we walk you or drive you or whatever?" Harry asked, hopeful.

"Er, well …"

"You all live close?" George asked.

"Well, we do as it happens," Billie nodded. "Kemp Town, just a mile or so."

"Where you parked?" Jon asked the boys.

"Square round the back here, I think," Harry replied vaguely.

"Not up by the station then?"

"No."

"Should be OK. There are a couple of biker cafés up that way."

"That where you are then?" Billie asked.

"Near there, yeah."

"Well, the Whiskey A Go-Go is just over the way here on Queen's Square," she said, pointing out through the windows to somewhere up past the Clock Tower. "But if you make your way round to the left you can miss it. There's then a smaller place to get by on Dyke Road, Tingeys. But it's an older guys place. They'll not be that bothered. You can nip through the church."

"Billie, what would we have done without you," Jimmy smiled.

"Aw, don't be dumb. You saved me, not the other way round."

"Bit of both," Jimmy suggested. "Take care of them guys," he added for the cousins.

"No question. And we'll see you in two weeks?" Paul checked.

"Will do. You wanna bring your kid brother?" Jimmy asked of Jon, adding for the others: "Jon's brother's got a band going at school."

"Yeah, bring him along. Get there early and he can jam a while if he wants," Paul offered.

"Really? Thanks. I reckon he'd like that," Jon nodded. "And you," he added for Jimmy, "should bring your sister. We'll make a proper family thing of it, brothers, cousins, sisters …"

"Deal."

"Cool," Paul beamed.

Jimmy, Charlie and Jon watched as the four guys and three girls made their way through the tables to the exit.

"What you think?" Charlie asked.

"Who knows," Jimmy replied. "All I would say is they all seemed like really decent people, don't you think?"

"Totally, no doubt. Makes you feel good, doesn't it, when you meet nice people."

"Yeah …" Jimmy mused. "Puts things in perspective."

"So what happened to Odysseus?" Jon asked.

"Vanessa," Jimmy sighed.

"Oh no! What a fucking idiot …"

"She that slag that was with Billie?" Charlie asked.

"That's the one," Jon nodded. "She know?"

"I reckon. Manny said he'd tell Dawn and see … but, well I caught her eye a while ago. I'd say they've told her something, bound to have really."

"So that's why you've been hiding over here with us," Charlie smiled. "Keeping out the way?"

"I guess," Jimmy nodded sheepishly.

"Well I hope you hurt him, useless fuck," Jon rasped.

"Some, I suppose …"

"Yeah, well …" Jon sighed more thoughtfully. "Tough on you, though, I suppose. Easy for us to say the prat's a tosser, but he was still your mate …"

"Was Jon, past tense. Was once, but people move on."

"Talking of which," Charlie nudged Jon. "Think we should get scarce for a moment."

"What?" Jon asked blankly before seeing Penny getting out of her chair. "Oh yeah, too right. Let's, er … jukebox, I think," he suggested, getting up.

"Sorry, what you on about?" Jimmy asked dumbly.

"Be cool kid," Charlie advised, getting up also. "Oh, Penny," he smiled with exaggerated charm. "Me and Jon were just going to feed the jukebox. Any requests?"

"Hmm, not sure … see if there's any Motown, or something soulful."

"No problem."

"You OK?" Penny asked, looking down into Jimmy's slightly sad eyes, an inquisitive, pensive look across her pretty face.

"Course, sure," he replied, trying for super-cool-nothing-fazes-me. "You?"

"Fine. I'm fine Jimmy," she nodded, sitting in the chair next to him, still staring into his eyes.

"They told you?" he asked.

"Yeah," she grimaced ruefully. "They told me. Well, kind of …"

"Eh?"

"Well, Pete filled it out for Manny, he told Dawn, she told me. So chances are I've heard it all back-to-front," she laughed dryly.

"OK. Yeah, well …" Jimmy replied uncertainly, looking down at the table, needing a break from her intent yet fathomless gaze.

"Yeah well," she echoed.

"So … what you going to do?" he asked after a moment, still unable to look at her, his fingers knitting together nervously.

"Do? Nothing," she replied. "What's to do?"

"Oh, yeah, right …"

"I mean," she continued, her hand resting gently on his arm, "I think we were drifting anyway, you know, lately. He's … well, while I gotta admit I would have preferred a less insulting end. An end's an end. No point fretting."

"I guess …"

"Jimmy, look," she said, a more earnest, considerate tone to her voice, a more caring sense to her touch. "I know you and he have been friends a long time. If, you know, after a few weeks you and he … well it won't be my concern, not my …"

"No Penny," he interrupted, his eyes suddenly drawn back to hers. "That won't happen. Bit like you said, we've drifted too. People change, he's changed. I … well, the bottom line is: I don't need people around me I can't respect."

"Aren't you moral?" she smiled.

"You think that's wrong?" he asked, confused by the amused look now brightening her face.

"Of course not, you dope!" she laughed. "How can that be wrong. You're a decent guy Jimmy Carlton. That's good!"

"Oh, yeah, well …" he blushed shyly.

"Look at you with that girl earlier, Billie."

"What about her."

"You know full well she would have thrown herself all over you if you'd let her. So what d'you do? You ease her down and find her a couple of decent people to be friends with. That's classy."

"You think?" he beamed proudly, optimistically.

"Yes, I do," she nodded, patting his arm, then lifting her hand away as she sat back, smiling contentedly. "I like this song," she said, gently letting her head roll in time to Otis Redding's *You Send Me*. "And I like them," she added, looking down to the jukebox to see Jon and Charlie looking back, miming along with their hands held out, palms up, like Otis' backing singers.

"They're good guys," Jimmy agreed, laughing at the girly way the two of them mimed: *honest you do, honest you do, honest you do*, one hand still held out, the other clamped over their hearts.

"The end of this thing with Mikey," Penny sighed, her eyes serious once more. "I don't want that to mean I lose touch with all of you," she insisted, nodding up towards Jon and Charlie, then down towards Manny and the rest.

"But ..." Jimmy began, his mind a mess of confusion and misunderstanding. "Why should it? I mean, of course not. Who would want it to?"

"I was just saying," she smiled, a hint of shyness in the blush reddening her cheeks. "In case there was any doubt."

"Penny, we like you. We all like you. That's why ..."

"That's why you hit O'Dea," she nodded, more like a summary than a question.

"Well, yes," Jimmy replied blankly. "I mean ..." he started while still thinking. "I was just going to say, why else," he smiled wryly. "But there is more to it. OK, yes I hit him because you deserve better than that ..."

"Thank you."

"And so do the rest of us too. Shit like him, acting like that - and earlier, hiding away and all that - you let someone who isn't decent hang around in your life and they suck the decency from you."

"That more greek stuff?" she asked, indulgent and impressed.

"You know what," he laughed. "I'm not sure. Think I might have just made that up myself!"

"Well good for you," she smiled appreciatively. "And for what it's worth, I actually think I understand. The difficult thing is, I guess, recognising the change. Admitting the moment when someone you thought decent has changed. I mean, I guess we always end up giving them a second and third chance out of, what, loyalty? Something like that …"

"That's why it's good to let new people in every now and then," Jimmy interrupted.

"You mean like Jon and Charlie?"

"Them? Yeah, for sure …"

"How long you known them?"

"A few months, but …"

"That's enough," she suggested, her head titled to one side.

"Yeah, I think."

"You know, I reckon sometimes you know in minutes. I've not spoken much to that Charlie, so I take him on trust. But Jon, you can tell straight off he's a decent guy."

"He is …" Jimmy replied, an unbecoming shaft of jealousy making his reply just a little stilted.

"Just like you," she added, for the avoidance of doubt.

"Hmm," he smiled, warmed by those sun-gold halos shining in her eyes. "Actually," he continued. "I was going to say, those kids we've been talking to …"

"The two that took care of Billie?"

"Yeah, them. And their cousins. And the two girls they were with … all really decent people, you know …"

"So, we lose one little shit, gain a whole new tribe," she suggested.

"Yeah," he agreed happily. "And, what's more, that Paul's in a band. They've got a gig in a couple of weeks down in Bexley. Said we'd all go."

"Good for you."

"You should come to," he added, partly as a question but with other hopes in mind. Hopes that instantly made him blush, made him babble on to cover himself. "Bring Toby. Jon's bringing his kid brother, who's also got a band. I said I'd take Janey, 'bout time I showed more interest …"

"I wonder what she'll make of Sally," Penny mused breezily.

"Wonder what …" Jimmy repeated, his body suddenly tense.

"She likes you, you realise that don't you?"

"Well, yeah, I guess …"

"Yeah, I guess," Penny repeated, laughing teasingly. "Like: girls fall for me, what can I do?" she smiled, holding her hands out in a feigned apology.

"I didn't mean that."

"Why not, it's probably true," she grinned. "Just like Billie. But anyway, that was what I wanted to say earlier. Sally, she's a bit all over the place because of it. You know, thought it would just be a fling, bit of fun, but …"

"She … told you all this?"

"Mostly, rest I worked out. She's my friend, Jimmy. I do understand her you know."

"Yes, of course," he acknowledged slowly, a ray of unanticipated and decidedly unwelcome light brightening a shadowy corner of his mind.

He hadn't thought, had he. Simply hadn't stopped to think about the complicated tapestry of friendships and loyalties that make life confusing, difficult. That make doing the right thing by the right people easier to say than pull off. That make it so hard to see the totality of any moment or thing or person. We only ever see bits of life, don't we. Only ever see it from one place, like Descartes' horse.

Everything slowed right down as he tried to think. *Boom Boom* started up from the jukebox but it sounded like one of his grandmother's 78s played at 33, slurred and sort of otherworldly.

She's my friend echoed around his brain, like a scream in those caves he visited on a school trip. Where were they? Had to get a train out of the city, past all those suburban stations with country-sounding names like Green, Park, Woods ...

She's my friend, of course she is. Mikey was his friend, Penny was his girl, Sally was her friend. What kind of a girl would makes eyes at a friend's guy? Well, someone like that Vanessa, obvious enough. But Penny, of course not.

She's my friend, Jimmy.

"Just as I thought," Penny continued, her voice quiet, kind but serious. "You're not sure either. She knows, Jimmy - the age thing, the husband thing ... she's not stupid."

"I never said ..."

"No, of course you didn't. I didn't mean you'd even think it. I'm just saying ... what am I saying," she giggled as Charlie and Jon walked behind, strutting and singing along with John Lee Hooker:

"When you talking to me, that baby talk. I like it like that ..."

"As I was saying," she continued, a happy smile on her face. "There are lots of reasons why it might be difficult, might not work. She understands ... I just thought you should too."

"Yeah, right, OK," Jimmy nodded, the ache down his left side suddenly wrapping itself around his heart, suffocating his foolish, love-struck optimism while his dizzy mind got washed through with chilled realism.

She's my friend, Jimmy.

"You're a decent guy Jimmy, I know that. I really do. So all I'm saying is, if it's not going to happen, if it all looks too difficult … well honest, I would understand. But you do right by her, you hear me? You hurt her and I'll hurt you twice as much as anything you did to O'Dea. We clear?" she asked menacingly yet with the sweetest smile dancing across her lips, the warmest look of friendliness in those beautiful eyes.

"We're clear," Jimmy nodded, a thin smile playing on lips that he was powerless to prevent from trembling with a feeling of loss.

Chapter 8

Soon you'll be gone and I'll be all alone
Soon you'll be gone and I'll be all alone

Because I messed up, 'cos I fooled around
I'm gonna sleep right here in this ground
So give some mind, to my soul
To keep me warm when I get cold.

Soon You'll Be Gone
The Blues Busters

Working off Billie's advice, Jon and Charlie led the group left of the Clock Tower, away from the Whiskey A Go-Go. Then, going up through St Nicholas' churchyard, they missed Tingeys and made their way to the scooters parked near Electricity House. Whilst the air was sea-chilled, the redness rising somewhere behind the buildings to their right suggested the sun would soon warm them.

Which was just as well as far as Jimmy was concerned. Walking slowly at the back of the group, Pete and Keith on either side, he felt cold as well as numb. Numb physically, like ice emotionally.

She's my friend, Jimmy. Did that mean never? Well, she'd said she would understand if he and Sally didn't work out. But no way was that the same as saying she'd then be wanting to stress the ties between her and her friend. Or, for that matter, between her and him. What he and Sally were to each other was not for her to determine. What she was to each of them, however, was only for her to decide. And on reflection, he really did not see any good reason for her to want to choose between them.

When all was said and done, he'd done the right thing. He and Mikey had to fall out because Mikey was a shit. Fine, end of as far as that clown was concerned.

But other than that, nothing else had changed. The joys, loyalties and complications of friendship were, as always, intertwined. Penny was his friend, just that. Like Manny and Dawn and Pete were his friends. Like Sally was now a friend for them. Like Jon and Charlie were becoming also.

He rode on the back of Charlie's scooter this time, an LD150 like his but in a pretty crappy condition. The engine sounded like a lawn-mower, the single mirror was pitted, the green paintwork scratched and faded, and the cushion-less back rest felt as comfortable as iron railings. Other than that it was fine! More than that, it was still a better option than Jon's, the second seat to which had springs poking through!

He'd had to let Penny ride on the TV, of course he had. And let Toby ride with Pete, only right and decent thing a man could do.

As they cruised down past the Whiskey A Go-Go - no need to avoid it on wheels - he laughed at the predicability of the music pouring out through the open door. Gene Vincent. Bet their jukebox has got nothing but Vincent, Cochrane and Presley, he thought. Don't those guys get bored?

Clearly the place was just as much an all-nighter as the Zodiac. There were still plenty of bikes parked up outside. Lots of Triumphs and Nortons, a 650 Thunderbird, a big american Harley, a BSA A7 - hadn't he seen that earlier?

A couple of ugly geezers in waxed Belstaff Trialsmaster jackets gave them some verbal, but what the fuck. Jimmy couldn't be bothered to acknowledge them, thinking afterwards that ignoring them was probably the most hurtful thing he could have done. Good!

As they rode along Marine Parade towards the Pavilion the sun was rising into his face, making his eyes narrow and blink. Making weirdly wonderful blobs of colour and shards of silverly glass dance in his brain.

Weirdly wonderful colours danced also around the onion domes and minarets, while the conical clown's hat seemed to be sparkling with a teasing, mocking madness all of its own.

He tried to relax as they headed north. Tried to will his head to stop aching. Tried to coax his numb body into some kind of life. But the crisp air was cutting through him, cooling his blood, chilling his bones. His feet especially felt icy, them and his fingers. He wanted to reach for another heart, he was sure there was at least one left in the little envelope. But no matter how hard he concentrated he just couldn't make his arm move.

And then a new feeling swept through him. A feeling of ennui, of couldn't care less, of what the fuck. With a glassy, unblinking stare he watched the world slip by in a dewy, raw, bitter blur. All the excitement of the planning and imagining was a long faded emotion. All the thrill of the fighting a distant memory. Even the super-charged tingle of that dance with Penny was now little more than a dying spark.

He felt hollowed out, devoid suddenly of optimism, of make-your-own-luck bravado, of one-day-Jimmy-boy certainty. *These arms of mine, they are lonely, lonely and feeling blue*, he sang to himself, silent and slow.

He had no idea whose idea it had been to stop. Not Charlie's, seeing as they were at the back. Maybe Penny's? Maybe Keith's and / or Pete's? - the two of them wanting just to take another look at the damage and make sure the thing was safe till they could get down with the truck. Who cares.

With some difficulty - and discomfort - he got off the scooter and followed the others across the road. Then, without any warning, as they reached his trashed scooter, he fainted.

"I told you, I fucking told you," he heard Penny saying. Told me what, he tried to say. You told me she's your friend. I get that. I told you I get that. We're cool, everything's cool. No need to worry. As soon as we get back home I'll call Sally. Maybe she and I will last a good while. We'll see. But whatever, we'll stay friends. We'll all stay friends.

"Yeah, he's coming round now," Manny said.

"Thank fuck," Charlie sighed.

OK guys, OK. Don't make a drama out of it. I fell over, big deal! You never fall over? Jesus, it's not like anyone's died for fuck's sake!

Now, where was I? Oh yeah. So, I'll go talk to Sally, it'll be cool. And she'll come to the Black Prince thing too, meet Janey. They'll like each other, of course they will. Janey will love it all so much. Being out with Sally and Penny. Meeting Paul's band, maybe those dudes with Graham Bond … what a stupid name they've got, the Organisation! Who the fuck they think they are? Makes Epitaphs Soul Band sound sensible. Maybe she'll get on with Jon's kid brother, bet the little guy's a ringer for his brother. Yeah, make the match Jimmy, make the match.

"Anyone got any water or anything?" Mikey asked.

Where the fuck did he come from? What the fuck is he doing here? What is this? And how did the sun get so high so quickly?

"Come on man," he heard Jon say.

"OK, OK," he gasped, spurting water over Jon's coat.

Suddenly, the sun was pouring through the gaps between all those heads forming a circle above him, making their faces disappear into a shadowy blackness. Contra jour, against the day, faces as blank as the night, voices as soft and warm as cotton wool.

Warm, comforting voices cooing around him, wrapping him up, telling him everything's going to be alright, everything's going to work out just so great. Voices like an expensive, woven cloth, wrapping around his numb, motionless body.

He looked up into those blank faces, trying to smile, trying to agree: yes, everything's going to be alright. He tried to tell them how thankful he was they were there for him. How very much better he felt now that Penny too had laid her coat across him.

But he couldn't move his lips. And more than that, he couldn't look at the sun any more. It was hurting his eyes. Maybe he'd feel better after a little sleep. Yes, that was all he needed, just a few moments of shut eye. Yes, that would do it. A little hibernation maybe, let his heart slow down.

Yes, that's fine Penny, pull the coat up. Cover my eyes while I just sleep a little while.

Chapter 9

There is a young cowboy
He lives on the range
His horse and his cattle
Are his only companions
He works in the saddle
And sleeps in the canyons
Waiting for summer
His pastures to change.

Goodnight you moonlight ladies
Rockabye sweet baby James
Deep greens and blues
Are the colours I choose
Won't you let me go down in my dreams
And rockabye sweet baby James.

Sweet Baby James
James Taylor

Penny parked in the small lay-by. Up ahead the sun was just peeping through a small copse on the hill on the horizon. Then, as if those trees had been waiting for this moment, they let their branches bend a little in the wind, allowing the sun to shine through, filling the car with a warming, ethereal, orange glow. She gazed recklessly into the light, narrowing her eyes to tiny slits, open just enough to let the star's spirit calm her mind.

"Was it here?" Jane asked.

"Just there, on that bend," Penny nodded sadly, still looking straight ahead, unable to look at Jimmy's sister, sensing with delicate acuity the heartache testing the young woman's nerve.

"It's just … it's just so … ordinary."

"I … I really don't know how it happened …"

"Manny said they were singing."

"That's what Jon said. He and Charlie had joined up with us on the way down. I can't remember where, somewhere. That was how it was, people joining up all the time."

"They came round the next day," Jane said, her voice weak, barely a whisper, like every word was an effort. "Came with Manny and Pete. Said they'd known Jimmy from some club?" she half recalled, half questioned, a sob choking her throat.

"Yeah, they …" Penny began, finding the courage to turn and look at Jane. Seeing the tears starting to form in her sad, blue eyes. Her pretty face paled with tension. "They were so upset, the two of them. Crying. We all were. I mean …" she started to babble, a tear trickling from her own right eye now. "It was dreadful, dreadful, dreadful …" she sobbed. "He was just such a lovely guy, your brother. Such a lovely, lovely guy …" she managed to say before her resolve fled. Before the tears started to fall more heavily. Before she gave in, crying like she had that day.

Seven years ago to the day.

"Penny, thank you," Jane said through her own sobbing, a thin smile trying so hard to linger on her lips.

"Wh-what for?" Penny asked, wiping away tears that would not stop.

"For bringing me here. I … I needed to see. See for myself. I miss him so much."

"I know, I know … we all do. But you … you were so young. Oh god, Jane, not a day passes when I don't wish …"

"It's … it's OK," Jane insisted, reaching out to comfort Penny, patting the back of her hand still stuck grippingly around the gear knob. "No-one's to blame, I know that."

"Does your mum?"

"She does … For ages she wouldn't say so. Blamed that Michael, not sure why but I guess she never liked him. She was OK-enough when he used to come round. And at the funeral. But she didn't like him. Did blame him."

"You know I haven't seen or heard of him in years."

"No, nor have we. I'm not sure who has. But mum, she did trust Manny - she was at school with his mum …"

"Really, I didn't know that," Penny smiled, comforted by the familiarity of family ties and long-held friendships.

"And Pete of course. He and Jimmy had known each other since before they could walk. They …" Jane paused, looking ahead to the so tame and innocent-looking bend for a moment while wiping away more tears. "Well, like you said, they told her and my dad again and again that it was no-one's fault, not even Jimmy's, though you can't be sure, can you? I mean, he must have lost concentration, don't you think. Thinking about something else and then …"

"He was talking about you, that day."

"Me, really?"

"Yeah, we stopped so often I can't tell you where we were. That journey must have taken us three, maybe four hours. We kept pulling in to meet up with different people, it was …" Penny sighed, breathing deep and hard to maintain her composure. "Yeah, well I guess we should have stopped more. But like I said, he was chatting about you, saying you were going to be a writer or something."

"He said that?"

"Yeah, why, not true?"

"Who knows," Jane laughed. "I'm going to be a teacher, see how that goes. But actually …"

"Yes?"

"We spoke about that, about writing, on the day. At breakfast."

"Oh, well guess that's why it was in his head."

"I guess," Jane smiled thinly, thoughtfully. "I remember everything about that morning. Every word. Every gesture. Every … it's all I have Penny," she sighed, sobbing once more.

"I know, I know."

"Who was the girl?"

"Sorry?"

"Mum said she'd seen you a day or so before and you'd said Jimmy was seeing some girl you worked with?"

"Did I say that? Yeah, well, girl … not really a girl …"

"What? You saying our Jimmy was queer!"

"What! Don't be daft," Penny laughed, pushing playfully at Jane's arm. "No, Sally, she was … well, she was quite a bit older than the rest of us. You're right though, I did work with her."

"No more?"

"No …" Penny pondered for a moment. "You see, the thing is, Sally … well, she was married. Her husband was a printer, worked nights …"

"No!" Jane gasped, covering her horrified mouth with her palm.

"She did come to the funeral. She was nice, I mean, you know, a really nice person. I said I'd introduce you but she didn't think that would be right. So she stood at the back and then left. Didn't come down your dad's club afterwards."

"Wow, the little …" Jane giggled. "Pity she didn't say something. You don't see her now?"

"No." Penny shook her head. "About a year later they moved, her and her husband. Up to Peterborough I

think. Somewhere like that. Lots of new jobs there were
..."

"Jimmy said she was a time traveller ..."

"Really?" Penny asked, pulling a confused face. "Not sure what that meant."

"Oh nothing. He was just joking around. My dad said something like when we gonna see this girl of yours and he said he couldn't be sure, she was like Doctor Who. All over the place in time."

"What your dad say?"

"Said Jimmy should buy her a watch!" Jane smiled.

"Good answer!"

"Yeah! Mum was teasing him about you though."

"Your father?"

"No, Jimmy," Jane laughed. "Kept saying how nice you were. How she thought you and he ... well, like I said, she didn't like Michael O'Dea. What happened with you and him?"

"Oh, nothing really. I mean, nothing 'happened' as such. He just wasn't 'the one'. We were OK for a while but ... well, I guess, if I'm honest, I did blame him for Jimmy. He was the one that wanted us all to go down that day. Some macho crap about getting back for the barney at Clacton ... stupid arse."

"Yeah, well ... mum said you were too good for him!"

"Did she," Penny smiled acceptingly. "Perceptive woman, your mother! But I guess Jimmy liked him, they were mates, that counted. He used to refer to Mikey as Odysseus."

"Really?"

"Some Greek hero, that right?"

"Well, yeah ..." Jane replied while thinking. "You know, it's maybe a bit more complicated than that. Jimmy didn't really rate Odysseus."

"Really?" Penny asked, feeling a little out of her depth. "I never could follow him when he talked about all that Greek stuff."

"No? It's simple really," Jane explained. "The big names, like Odysseus and Achilles, they were like Generals. Not Jimmy's kind of people," she continued with enthusiasm. "He thought real men were the guys who really fought. Not those who just talked a good fight. Guys like Diomedes and Patroclus ... sorry," she stopped, giggling self-consciously. "Am I losing you?"

"A bit!" Penny laughed. "You are so like him."

"Am I? Really?"

"Yeah, too clever by half!" Penny smiled. "But don't give it up. Nothing wrong with being clever Jane. Now I look back the problem was I just wasn't clever enough to understand him half the time."

"Wh-why? What you thinking?"

"One time - and I think it probably was only the once - we were talking about Mikey and I asked what that Odysseus thing was all about, thinking it was something as shallow as a play on the name. You know, O'Dea / Odysseus?"

"Hmm," Jane grinned ruefully.

"Yeah, well now I'm seeing," Penny nodded. "What he actually said was something like: you see, the problem with heroes is people only see how dim they are when it's too late."

"That's about the sum of it," Jane agreed.

"Is it?" Penny asked.

"Yep," Jane smiled, pausing a moment to stare out towards the sea. "So, was she right, my mum? She reckoned you were sweet on our Jimmy," she laughed teasingly, knowingly discomforting Penny.

"I ..." Penny started, honesty and dissimulation battling politely in her mind. "Yes ..." she sighed, accepting the wisdom of honesty. "I only met him through Mikey of course. That was always in the way. But we did get on. We used to meet occasionally for a coffee after work. There was this Italian place he really liked in Cannon Street, had a great jukebox …"

"You worked near each other, right?"

"Yeah, like two streets away. He brought me home one time, late I mean. We'd both had Christmas parties the same night so he said he'd meet me on the corner of Cheapside. We got on a bus full of drunks and idiots but with Jimmy …" Penny smiled, comforted now by a happy memory. "With him I just felt so safe. Like I said Jane, your brother was just a very special guy."

"Yeah," Jane nodded, looking at Penny intently. Thinking, wishing that maybe in some parallel universe there was another Penny and Jimmy living a nice life surrounded by lovely children, the nieces and nephews she was never going to know. "You know, it's sort of because of him that I'm going to teach."

"Really, he suggested that?"

"No, not as such. Months later my dad sat down with me, all serious like. I thought it was going to be another intense lecture, he was so obviously petrified still by a fear that something would happen to me next. But it wasn't that …" Jane remembered, watching Penny watching her, listening so attentively. "It was again something to do with that last day. Jimmy evidently told him he should talk to me. Say something to show it would make him proud, you know, if I did well at school. Went to university. That sort of thing. But of course, he got all choked up so ended up making me think he was saying I should do all that for Jimmy."

"He was clever, wasn't he."

"Jimmy? Yeah," Jane smiled. "Oh yeah … it was a couple of years later my dad managed to tell me what he'd really been trying to say. Jimmy had told him to say that stuff, but in hearing it my dad had asked why he'd not wanted to stay on at school, go to university himself. He said something like he kind of talked himself out of it. Convinced himself that boys from Peckham didn't do that sort of thing. He didn't regret it, but at the same time he didn't want me thinking the same, ending up in a shop or something …"

"He was proud of you Jane, that's so obvious. I thought it then, when he talked about you. But it's even clearer now."

The two women sat in silence for a few moments, each staring up towards the scene of the crash, lost in their different thoughts and memories of the same guy.

"Did you say where you're going to teach?" Penny asked uncertainly.

"Oh yeah," Jane burst with renewed spirit. "Well, you know, first off I thought I ought to try my old school. Peckham girl not done too bad and all that. I thought I might show the girls there today that there's a world of opportunity waiting for them too."

"And?"

"I got turned down!" Jane laughed, a trace of anger flashing in her eyes.

"That's such crap," Penny rasped. "So where are you going?"

"Well, near you I think. Chislehurst?"

"Never! That's just up the road. Where?"

"The girls' grammar?"

"I know it. It's like a mile from us. Hardly any more. We're actually quite close to the boys' school, in Sidcup."

"Oh right, yeah. That's the school's name: Chislehurst & Sidcup."

"So where you going to live? You going to travel from home?"

"Not sure …" Jane pondered. "I mean, I've been away, apart from hols, for nearly four years now. Not sure I want to go back full-time."

"You could stay with us," Penny suggested tentatively.

"No," Jane laughed. "I wasn't fishing for that. The school's given me a list of people they know rent out rooms. I just need to find the time …"

"No Jane, I'm serious. We've got a big enough house. Like I said, we're only down the road. You can have a couple of rooms actually."

"No Penny, honestly …" Jane replied without meaning it.

"Right, that's settled then!" Penny laughed. "Look, I really mean it. Just do it for the first year, till you've got a bit of money behind you. It would be lovely. And I think you'll like it. I liked Peckham well enough when I lived there, but I couldn't go back, not now. It's changed … and changing," she considered. "Plus, you can babysit!"

"Oh great …"

"He's no trouble."

"Actually, I could do that no matter where I end up," Jane smiled, "I'd like to."

"He's lovely. Bet every mother says that!"

"About their sons? Yep!"

"Yeah, well …" Penny sighed, the grim reality of why they were there creeping back in. "Come on."

They got out of the car, collected their bunches of fresh flowers from the boot and walked along the side of the road to the spot. As they laid the flowers down Penny pulled Jimmy's sister to her, hugging the girl while she wept. Weeping herself as she always did.

"Thank you, again," Jane whispered.

"Well, I was coming anyway."

"You said."

"I've come every year. Well save two years back when I was eight months pregnant. Manny, Pete and Keith come down every year too. For the first couple of years we all came together in Alfie Bowles' truck. Classy!" Penny shrugged ruefully.

"That's so nice, so kind."

"And it was here, of course, that I met Jon again. The third year. I had a car then. I was standing here alone, crying. He and Charlie pulled up in this purple Mini he'd just bought - he's still got it. Shit, did we blub."

"Jimmy brought you together," Jane nodded, a sweet and happy smile on her lips.

"He did, Jane, he did. And he'll always be with us now …"

"Sweet baby James," Jane smiled. "I can't wait to meet him again. He's obviously grown lots since the christening …"

"In every way," Penny nodded. "Got a mess of hair just like his dad …"

"I love that James Taylor song too."

"Tell me about it. Jon sings it to him several times a day!" Penny laughed.

"Got love if you want it," Jane mused randomly after a moment's silence.

"Sorry?"

"I've just thought, I bet that was the song they were singing," Jane suggested. "I'd forgotten it till recently. Last Christmas my mum suddenly decided we could clear Jimmy's room. It'd just been left. No-one went in there but her. She and I did it on his birthday. It was horrible. But amongst the things I kept was that record, by someone called Slim Harpo. He loved it. Used to play it over and over. Bet that's what they were singing …"

"You can check with Jon when you move in!"

"I'll bring it with me."

"Do … got love if you want it. Don't that just sum him up."

"OK, I'm done now," Jane sighed, her spirit lifted by the closeness she felt once more to her brother.

"Me too … you see this field here," Penny nodded as they walked back to the car, pointing across to a verdant slope of lush grass running down from the copse. "There were horses in it that year. Four or five of them. Wild, running free … then they stopped, stood staring at us. I like to think they carried his spirit off, after we left. He would have liked that."

"He would have, no question."

I know I've dreamed you
A sin and a lie
I have my freedom
But I don't have much time
Faith has been broken
Tears must be cried
Let's do some living
After we die

Wild horses, couldn't drag me away
Wild wild horses, we'll ride them someday.

Wild Horses
Rolling Stones

Notes

The idea of a narrative imagined in a dying man's final moments has been explored by a few authors. The first to do so, as far as I am aware, was Ambrose Bierce in his short story *An Occurrence at Owl Creek Bridge* (1890). I certainly acknowledge a debt to this excellent work, which deserves a new readership.

The significant difference between Bierce's Peyton Farquhar and Jimmy Carlton though, is this: Peyton's focus is essentially survival, cheating the hangman to get home to his wife and children; Jimmy's is a quest for honour - which makes it also a trial of his character, a test of his determination to do the right thing for the right reason.

Many have drawn on Homer's *Iliad* and *Odyssey* for plot and characters. My favourite by far is James Joyce's *Ulysses*, which I happily acknowledge as an influence. Again, though, with differences.

Joyce deliberately created a non-heroic figure in the Odysseus role, a man longing still for a wife who is anything but a virtuous Penelope. Jimmy isn't Odysseus, he is Diomedes.

And for good reason: when all is said and done Odysseus may be favoured by the gods, but he is an inconstant friend, none too bright and a pretty useless leader!

The influence of *The Odyssey* on Jimmy's story is as follows:

- Chapter 2 - his sense of drowning echoes Odysseus in Book V (after being thrown from a boat in Poseidon's storm). It is from this single connection that Jimmy's dying mind creates, using a sequence of scenes remembered from *The Odyssey*, a story of him living to make his own journey towards a kind of glory. He actually dies shortly after gasping: "OK, OK" (pp. 29 / 134).

- Chapter 3 - Brighton Pavilion is the Palace of Alcinous, Book VII.
- Chapter 4 is basically the Phaeacian Games, Book VIII, with some debt also to Book V of *The Iliad*, Diomedes Fights The Gods. In the goading of O'Dea, Jon and Charlie are Euryalus and Laodamas.
- Chapter 5 - the Istanbul is the house of Aeolus on Aeolia, Book X; and the name Cilla is a play on Circe. The call Pete, Toby and Charlie cannot resist is that of the Sirens, Book XII.
- Chapter 6 is the post-Games feast at Alcinous' Palace, Book VIII. Insofar as Jimmy has an inspiration for his dance with Penny, it has to be Halius and Laodamas. That said, the scene as written owes a considerable debt to Vincent Vega (John Travolta) and Mia Wallace (Uma Thurman) in Quentin Tarantino's *Pulp Fiction*. Partly for their sheer sexiness. But also because of the obvious parallel in the two couples' relationship. The death of the boy falling from the roof echoes that of Elpenor, Book X.
- Chapter 7 - the Zodiac stands for Aeaea, the Island of the Rising Sun, although they do not see the dawn until they leave. The purpose of this chapter is to provide a bridge (metaphor: the walk across roofs) between the implications of O'Dea's betrayal of Penny and her obvious - although until then not consciously considered by Jimmy's dying mind - loyalty to Sally. By intention, this is the chapter that makes Jimmy a tragic hero, one doomed by his own flaws to fail.
- Chapter 8 - the Whiskey A Go-Go and Tingeys stand here as Scylla and Charybdis, Book XII. Once past these the group start the journey home, or to Ithaca, Book XIII.

The main works of philosophy to influence the dialogues are: Boethius' *Consolation of Philosophy* and Aristotle's *Nicomachean Ethics.* There is also some Nietzsche in the argument about making your own luck and not harbouring regret.

In addition to interesting memories posted on blogs and records of contemporary interviews, I drew on Terry Rawlings' *Mod: Clean Living Under Very Difficult Circumstances - A Very British Phenomenon* for details on the mood, language, music and obsessions of May, 1964.

The soundtrack to this story is as follows:

- *Got Love If You Want It* - Slim Harpo / The Kinks
- *Don't Start Me Talking* - Sonny Boy Williamson
- *Come On* - Chuck Berry
- *You Really Got A Hold On Me* - Smokey Robinson
- *Al Capone* - Prince Buster & The All Stars
- *House Of The Rising Sun* - The Animals
- *I'm A Man* - John Lee Hooker
- *Dust My Broom* - Elmore James
- *Smokestack Lightning* - Howlin' Wolf
- *Respectable* - The Isley Brothers
- *Got My Mojo Working* - Muddy Waters
- *So Many Roads, So Many Trains* - Otis Rush
- *Louie Louie* - The Kingsmen
- *Yeah, Yeah* - Georgie Fame
- *Soon You'll Be Gone* - The Blues Busters
- *You Send Me* - Otis Redding
- *Boom, Boom* - John Lee Hooker
- *These Arms Of Mine* - Otis Redding
- *My Generation* - The Who
- *Sweet Baby James* - James Taylor
- *Wild Horses* - Rolling Stones

And some other stuff:

- Sunday, 17 May 1964. The first 'Mods and Rockers' clash to catch any kind of media attention took place seven weeks earlier at Clacton (Easter Monday, 30 March). The various repeats over the Whitsun weekend - across a number of south coast towns, most significantly Margate, Hasting and Brighton - were therefore somewhat arranged.

  Understandably, there was afterwards considerable public comment and disquiet - the towns were full of families and others enjoying a traditional Bank Holiday break. That this commentary then became increasingly puritanical - despairing of the values and attitudes of the young, especially their perceived disregard for law and order - owes much to the fact some of those involved on 17 May attacked the Police.

- The Roaring Twenties, on Carnaby Street, began as a black club playing ska and blue-beat. By 1964 it had become popular with white Mods, many of whom (especially those from east London) adopted a 'rude-boy' look of pork-pie hat, braces and tasselled loafers with white socks.

- The Scene was in Ham Yard, off Great Windmill Street in Soho. It occasionally hosted live bands but mostly it was a record-playing club with a reputation for breaking original, black american R&B. The DJ around 1964 was Guy Stevens.

- The 1945 Cup Final between Chelsea and Millwall was technically the South Final of the 1944-45 Football League War Cup. During the war most sport competitions were cancelled. Party because the nation's attention was obviously devoted to the war effort. But also because so many sportsmen joined their brothers and cousins in the Forces.

  Before the war Millwall had been one of the biggest and wealthiest clubs in the country. Not so, however, by 1964 - when they were relegated to the fourth division.

- 'The Dog' is the Crown & Greyhound. At the time it was arguably the best Young's pub in London, not least because for a while it was actually run by John Young before he took over as Chairman of the family firm later in 1964.

- The Crawdaddy - named after a Bo Diddley song - began at the Station Hotel before moving to the much larger Richmond Athletic Ground. The first house band was the hardly legendary Dave Hunt Rhythm & Blues Band - their footnote in history being that Charlie Watts played drums, Ray Davies guitar. The Rolling Stones took over the residency in March 1963, Watts having now joined them.

  Davies' Kinks stood in for The Stones a few times, but they never held the residency. That passed to The Yardbirds, at the time a bunch of unknowns from nearby Kingston.

- The guitarist in The Birds was Ronnie Wood, lately of course in the Stones. There was a bit of a copyright argument in 1964 over the name when The Byrds came to town.

- St Olave's Grammar School was, at the time, located in Queen Elizabeth Street near Tower Bridge. It moved to its current suburban home in 1968.

- The aerial connection between the Barn and Zodiac has been invented to fit the story. They, as well as the Istanbul, were favourite Mod places around 1964.

- The Whiskey A Go-Go was a favourite biker club from the 1950s onwards. Whilst not especially a place of trouble, it was central to a 1962 scandal. At the time it was owned by Harvey Holford. His wife had an affair with a wealthy local, John Bloom, as a result of which Holford shot her. He was given just a three year sentence on account, said the judge, of his wife's provocation and general loose behaviour.

- Tingey's was one of a few biker coffee bars in the town.

- The house band at The Barn was indeed called The Giants, led by a guy called Bobby Sansom.

- The Epitaphs Soul Band - long since forgotten - were briefly popular in south-east London, holding residencies at clubs in Bromley, Lewisham and Sidcup, as well as The Black Prince.

- The Black Prince regularly attracted top bands way into the 70s. Amongst others it was a favourite for both Eric Clapton and Ginger Baker (who lived nearby in New Eltham). In addition to the Yardbirds, an early Cream gig was played there, as well as one of the first by Derek and The Dominoes.

  Besides playing there with Graham Bond (whose bass player was Jack Bruce) Ginger Baker also took his Airforce there.

- The lyrics to Louie Louie aroused some controversy in 1964. Following a complaint from an outraged parent claiming The Kingsmen's version was obscene, the FBI conducted an investigation, concluding the lyrics were "unintelligible at any speed!"

  The words I've used are, as far as I am aware, those originally written by Richard Berry. The song tells the story of a Jamaican sailor thinking about his girl while trying to get home. Pretty much Odysseus' story, of course. And not too far from the imagined story in dying Jimmy's mind.

Printed in Great
Britain
by Amazon

31060559R00090